GAVIN

Immortal Highlander Book 5

HAZEL HUNTER

ALLURE PRESS

HH ONLINE

Hazel loves hearing from readers!
You can contact her at the links below.

Website: hazelhunter.com

Facebook:
business.facebook.com/HazelHunterAuthor

Newsletter: HazelHunter.com/news

I send newsletters with details on new releases,
special offers, and other bits of news related to
my writing. You can sign up here!

Chapter One

✦❖✦

THE PEARL-CAPPED sapphire waves of the North Sea lashed Gavin McShane as they buffeted the hull of the old boat. With practiced skill he guided the fisher into Scapa Flow, navigating his way through the boats and ships making passage between the islands that protected the wide but busy bay.

Overhead black wing-tipped gannets soared, diving now and then to scoop up fish to feed the screeching young waiting in their remote cliffside nests. Clear skies stretched wide and icy blue over the islands of Orkney, which resembled giant, rough-cut emeralds tumbling away from the north coast of Scotland. Gavin smiled a little as he passed other fishers that had yet to sail, or had returned with empty nets. Their crews cast envious looks at the mounds of cod heaped on the fisher's deck.

"See it and weep," Gavin murmured under his breath.

Being a twenty-first century man working on a medieval fishing boat had proven surprisingly satisfying. He no longer had to bother with phones, computers, cars, doctor's appointments, his walker or the disease that had been killing him in the future. Since time-traveling back to fourteenth-century Scotland, Gavin had enjoyed perfect health.

But he'd only achieved peace when he'd come to the islands.

Still, today's fine catch would pay his wages for three days, which would permit him the rest of the week to work on putting a roof on his house. He couldn't wait to finish it so he could move to Marr, the little jewel of an island he'd found off the coast of Hrossey.

"McShane," Bjarke Moller said as he came to join him at the helm. He was one of the three brothers who owned the boat. A burly man with strong arms roped by hard muscle and deep scars, he devoted himself to three pleasures in life: fishing, drinking and wenching. "Kron says you're no' to the alehouse with us. 'Tis true?"

"The salr needs work," Gavin replied. He now spoke without thinking in a thickened version of his natural brogue, but he still hesitated on some of the islander slang. But the salr—his house—was something he'd talked about for months. "I can drink any day. I cannae sleep in my salr without a roof."

"But you build on *Marr*, man?" That came from Silje Rowe, one of the net casters. The reedy, perpetually worried man touched the little wooden fish charm he wore around his neck. "No man goes near that island. 'Tis cursed."

"Och, aye, 'tis haunted by the ghost wench," Bjarke said and rolled his eyes. "She wears a torn blue gown and floats about the glen flashing her teats and arse. What does she now, steal men's souls or eat them? I cannae recall."

"Dinnae jest about the Blue Lady of Marr," Silje warned. He clutched his talisman tightly, and lowered his voice to a whisper.

"'Tis said she seeks vengeance for her tribe. They were massacred by blood-drinkers."

Gavin generally didn't mind listening to the fishermen's tall tales, but this one reminded him too much of the reason he had come to the islands to disappear. "I should see to the haul now."

"Aye, do," Bjarke said and took his place at the helm. "Silje, we're nearly to dock. Stop your havering and go ready the *vind-áss*."

Windlass, Gavin silently translated, the pulley and rope system they used to lift their heavy haul. When he'd first arrived in Orkney the islander's odd hodgepodge of Scottish and Norse had forced him to say little until he built a rough working vocabulary. He'd probably never learn all of the slang, so he focused on words related to fish, the sea, and his work on the boat.

The crew got busy as they docked by the fish monger's pier. Hoisting the burgeoning nets meant hand-cranking the windlass before they swung the cod over to empty them into waiting carts. Once the catch was offloaded, the men worked together as a brigade to sluice the upper deck clean with buckets of salt water. Then they hung the thistle-hemp nets to dry.

The day's tasks finished, the crew lined up to be paid by Bjarke, who promised them more work at the end of the week. As the newest deck hand Gavin was always the last to be paid. He had to trot to make the ferry that circled the bay to deliver people and supplies to the homes on the smaller islands. Gavin was the only one to disembark at Marr, and as he did he could feel the weight of the other passengers' gazes on his shoulders.

Stepping off onto the island's only dock, which was old but sturdy, he shouldered his pack and headed for the forest. Reaching the spot he'd chosen to build his house meant crossing the glen Silje claimed was haunted, although Gavin had never spotted anyone there. He liked to bathe in the fairy pool near the trees, and sometimes he jogged along the perimeter to stretch his legs. He'd been coming here for months and hadn't seen anything but deer, rabbits and the funny-looking broad-beaked puffins who nested on the rocks.

Whether the ghost stole souls or ate them, she didn't seem very interested in his.

The first sight of his half-finished cottage made Gavin feel an intense satisfaction. One dream he'd always had was to build a house with his own hands. As a teenager he'd landed a summer job as a gopher on a construction site, and soaked up everything the masons and carpenters were willing to teach him. Although the materials in the fourteenth century were much more primitive, he'd assumed the method would be the same: put down a strong foundation, build sturdy walls with framed openings for the windows and doors, and cap it off with a beamed roof.

Reality set in when his first attempt at building had collapsed it on itself while he'd been off crewing for the Moller brothers.

Gavin didn't waste any more time making assumptions. He'd learned which of his crewmates had built their own houses, and grilled them for details. That garnered him an invitation to visit Silje's home on Hrossey, where the net caster was working on an addition for his growing family. After meeting his crewmate's five children, along with his shy and very pregnant wife, Gavin could see why he needed the extra space.

"Why do you build two walls?" Gavin had asked as he inspected the double structures framing the new room.

"They become one wall when I fill the space between them with earth and rock. The thickness keeps out wind and cold, and makes the walls stronger." Silje pointed to the curving timbers he'd lashed together in the shape of a capital A. "Between the fill I stack red stone, with a hollow in the very top fitted to the ends of the roof beams. They need to stay in place if they are to hold the roof."

Gavin offered to help the net caster finish the addition, and spent another month in his free time getting the hands-on experience he needed to start over on his own cottage. It proved to be hard but satisfying work. Silje explained everything he did, and even demonstrated how to properly carve fitted wooden joints, weave denser thatching, and make clay mortar stronger by adding dried grass and crushed shells. All the work had to be done with only the most basic of tools and no hardware at all, but Gavin eventually began to appreciate how resourceful the islanders were.

As the children got to know him, he often found himself the center of their attention. Little sword fights with the boys and rides on his back for the girls soon became a treasured part of the day. When he'd been young, Gavin had just assumed he'd have a family. ALS had cut off that possibility. But now he even took up drawing again to surprise Silje's wife with sketches of her children.

"You're an odd one, McShane," the net caster said when they finished pinning the last bundle of thatching with bent willow twig spars, which to Gavin looked like large wooden staples. "I couldnae wheedle my cousin to come help a day, and here you do half the work for naught." He frowned. "Didnae your people build in the highlands?"

Gavin imagined telling his crewmate how houses would be built in seven hundred years. "They've a different way of it."

From the rocky shore of his own island Gavin sourced the weathered red sandstone for his foundation and walls, which he hauled to his building site on a handmade sled. Clay he dug and carried in buckets from the banks of the stream that snaked through the forest. The curved timbers for his roof came from trees growing on hill slopes. He used his earnings to purchase a hammer, ax and knife from the town blacksmith, and learned to whittle pins and pegs during lulls of work on the boat.

But he still made errors. He'd already learned that he was only a passable carpenter, and his masonry would never win any prizes. Even so he learned from every failure, and never made the same mistake twice. Now he had three days to place his roof frames over the cottage walls, and cover them with the thick panels of thatching he'd been weaving for weeks. He'd even constructed a ladder to give him better access to the top of the cottage.

The next time he came back to the island, it would be to live here, in this quiet, fragrant valley where everything was new and green and peaceful.

As Gavin approached the cottage he saw a flicker of movement at the back wall, where two of the island's small deer liked to graze on the sweet grasses that grew there. He dropped his pack deliberately to make noise, and the clank of his tools scared a pair of ducks into flight. He hadn't yet gone hunting on the island, preferring to bring his share of the day's catch or food he purchased on Hrossey. Once he moved into the cottage he'd have to start putting out snares, or stick to a seafood diet.

He'd hunted very successfully in the highland forests on the mainland, but he'd been hesitant to do the same here. All of the island's animals seemed remarkably interested in him, as if they'd never seen a man—or never been hunted.

The ducks he'd frightened away flew back around to perch atop his pile of building timbers. One was a striking black and white with a startling patch of green on its neck. The other had striped brown and cream feathers. A mated pair, Gavin decided, since they had the same wedge-shaped bill and bulky body shape. He'd seen others waddling in twos through the glen, probably hunting for safe nesting spots.

"You'll no' find a kindred spirit here," he told the ducks as he stripped off his jacket and rolled up the sleeves of his work tunic. "There'll be no wife or bairns coming to your island. 'Tis a bachelor's cottage I'm building."

Even when he was alone Gavin tried to speak in the heavy brogue of the islands. Somehow it made him feel more vital, and less like a dying cripple who had been flung through time to be cured and then nearly destroyed.

The ducks didn't seem impressed by his mastery of medieval speak, but they kept watching him as he checked his first roof beam assembly and set up the rope and wheel hoist to raise it over the walls.

The physical work of lifting two hundred pounds of timbers over his head made Gavin glad he'd built up plenty of muscle working for the Mollers. He'd never get tired of the pleasure of being strong again, not when he'd spent two years slowly wasting away in the prison his disease had made of his own body. Just before falling through time he'd lost the ability to walk without support. Now when he pulled on the rope hoist, the roof beam rose over him as if he'd built it from twigs.

He worked until the moon rose, and stars

glittered in the pale darkness that passed as night in the islands. By morning the mortar would set, and he could install the permanent cross beams that would provide more support for his roof.

The work left Gavin sweaty, grimy and tired, but he wouldn't trade the aches in his arms and shoulders for the world. After he unpacked the food he'd brought with him and ate a quick meal of smoked fish on black bread, he decided to go for a bath.

Hiking out to the spring near the center of the glen took time, but Gavin didn't mind the long walk. Too shallow for a soak, the water of the forest stream was also freezing cold. He'd discovered just the opposite when he'd seen steam rising from the glen's spring one morning, and walked over to inspect the crystal-clear waters. Somewhere under the jagged-edged, deep pool was a thermal pocket that kept it warm.

Once he reached the spring he stripped to the skin and jumped in. Being immersed in the heat immediately loosened his knotted muscles, and by the time he surfaced he felt utterly relaxed.

To Gavin's surprise he saw the two ducks had followed him from the cottage, and were now sitting on a flat rock as they watched him tread water.

"I cannae have pets," he told them as he swam over to the side and propped his arms on a long stone perfectly curved for that purpose. "I've no idea what ducks eat, and your lady there looks a bit plump. Does she eat for two, then?"

A strange tension at the back of his neck made him look around. But as he did the faintest floral scent drifted past his nostrils. Never one for gardening, Gavin had no idea what the flower he smelled might be, but it wasn't the first time. As it had on other occasions, the familiar aroma cast his mind back to the country farmhouse that he and Jema had shared. Though she'd enjoyed gardening, she never had the time. He smiled to himself as he remembered the slight young woman who'd accompanied their gardener. Jema had been thrilled with how the flower beds had bloomed under their care. Gavin had been content to watch the lass from his window.

The male duck made a muted squawking

sound that brought Gavin's attention back around. The bird stretched open his long beak as if he were yawning, and then nudged the female to her feet. They waddled off to disappear in the shadows.

Rejected again.

Gavin's smile vanished along with his good mood, and he climbed out of the pool. The moon silvered his tanned limbs and broad, ripped torso, and for a moment he looked like a ghost. Wasn't that what he'd become since his immortal lover Thora had betrayed him, and his twin sister Jema had left him for dead? A solitary specter of himself, playing at being a highlander-turned-fisherman—a joke of a man who had nothing and no one but himself.

He'd let go of his love for Thora. Nothing he could do would bring her back from the grave a second time. Even if he could, she'd never truly loved him. But missing Jema ate at him, for they'd been each other's best friends. Gavin knew he'd been a burden on her for years. Even though he was no longer sick his sister had started a fresh, new life with her Viking and his clan.

Discovering in one day that the two most

important women in his life had never really needed him had devastated Gavin. Coming to the islands to begin a new life had been the right decision. He could build a life for himself here. Maybe someday he'd meet someone who'd want to share it—an ordinary, healthy, fourteenth-century lass who wouldn't hold a blade to his throat as she betrayed him.

Chapter Two

✥

MIST SWIRLED AROUND Catriona Haral's clogs, chilling her toes and promising to veil the glen in heavy dew before sunrise. She glanced down at the eider ducks standing by her feet.

You've done well, she thought to them, and projected a memory of a sheltered niche she'd noticed near her village. *Go on with you, before the voles take it for their pups.*

The pair shook out their feathers and waddled off, eager to begin building the nest for their young. Catriona remained where she was and watched the highlander emerge from the spring.

Gods, but he was a massive, beautiful

beast. He stood tall and broad-shouldered and deep-chested, with dark, bronze hair that spilled over his shoulders. More dark hair pelted the bulging muscles of his torso. From the firm curves of his buttocks to the strong yoke of his upper shoulders, long, wide swaths of muscle padded his back, and swelled even bigger and heavier in his upper arms and thighs. She'd already seen him balance a huge log on one shoulder and carry it off, and wondered how many years he had labored to grow so powerful and confident.

Something about the highlander called to her, as she had not felt since her childhood. It had been so long ago she might be mistaken, but the man seemed to have other, hidden power, as if he were druid kind, like her.

Why would a druid work like an ox when he could use magic to ease his burdens? a little voice said inside her head. She sighed. *You see what you wish, not what 'tis there.*

Would the highlander be shocked to know she had been watching him for weeks? Or that just now, if she took three steps, she'd appear in front of him like a wraith made flesh? Would he run away shrieking like the other infrequent intruders that came to Everbay? Or would he attack her, beat her, or worse?

Because she couldn't answer those questions, Catriona stayed safely behind the barrier. Nor could she make a sound whenever the man came near her side of the island. The bespelled wall of magic that protected her and the village only prevented them from being seen. She'd had to leave several times since the highlander had come to Everbay, and each time she returned she found him still there.

He arrived every three or fiveday to work on his cottage, which he'd nearly finished. While he was away she'd done things to discourage his staying: scattering his tools, stealing his bedding, and knocking down his first attempt at building walls. It hadn't put him off, but watching how hard he worked to build better walls the second time left her feeling a curious mixture of pleasure and guilt.

The highlander knew little of island life, but he did not give up.

When he finished dressing the man headed back for his cottage, and Catriona paced him for the length of the glen. The barrier protecting her presence didn't extend into the forest, so she was obliged to stop at the tree line and watch the highlander from there until he disappeared from sight. Sometimes she considered waiting until he was asleep before she crossed through the spell boundary to see what progress he'd made on his house. Afraid of those unanswered questions, she sent the ducks or some of her other animal friends to spy on him.

Catriona didn't think having ducks and voles and deer as friends seemed odd, but she had been born with the ability to wordlessly communicate with them. Far more primitive in their thinking, animals mostly dwelled on their never-ending struggle to eat, breed and care for their young. They had more instincts than emotions, so they couldn't understand why she would sometimes curl up on her parent's old bed and weep for hours. All of the animals on the island regarded her as harmless if a little strange. The eiders had been quite happy to keep watch over the highlander while they looked for their nest, but with the female about to lay Catriona had to stop sending them after the man.

I should leave Everbay for good. Ennis and Senga

keep telling me 'tis too dangerous for me to dwell here alone, even with the barrier.

A twinge of guilt made her hunch her shoulders. She hadn't yet told her family about the highlander.

The scent of wood smoke lured Catriona to the very edge of the barrier, where she peered through the trees in vain. Pulling her dark cloak over her head, she stepped through and emerged on the highlander's side of the island. She quickly hid herself behind a tree, and waited while she listened for his heavy footsteps. When no sound came she darted to the next tree, and the next, until she saw his cottage.

Five arches of timber formed peaks over the rectangle of double stone walls, each braced in place. She smelled the fish he cooked even before she spied a seaweed-wrapped bundle on a flat stone in the center of the low ring of flames. He often brought with him strings of big sea cod which he always deftly cleaned, and sometimes stuffed with herbs and wild mushrooms. That and the darkening of his skin and small wounds on his hands and arms made her think he might be working at the docks, or on a fishing boat from the big island.

Tonight as his fish cooked the highlander sat with his back propped against a pine. Braced against his thighs lay a square of thin wood, on which he had placed a piece of parchment. He had something in his hand that he moved slowly back and forth over it, his brows drawn together over his storm cloud-colored eyes.

Whatever he did, it was not making him happy. His mouth had tightened so much it looked like a flat gash.

At last he put down the blackened bit of wood he'd been using, and stared at the parchment. "You're an idiot, Gav. Let her go."

Catriona jumped a little at the sound of his voice. Deep and soft, it stroked her very bones from within as it passed through her. Did he speak of himself? What sort of name was Gav, Norse? He looked proper Scottish to her. Why did he speak of holding a woman when he was alone here? She watched him turn the parchment to study it in the firelight. She gasped when he swore and flung it away. The parchment floated through the air to land only a few feet away from her.

In the bright moonlight she could see the fine drawing, which showed the face and shoulders of a woman. She had a pretty smile that didn't reach her eyes, and a hard line to her jaw that spoke of determination. The highlander had captured something so bleak in the sketch that Catriona felt an answering despair in her heart.

Had the lovely, hard-eyed woman lost everything? Was that why she looked as Catriona sometimes felt, as if she might go mad with grief?

She froze as the highlander strode over and snatched up the drawing. Not daring to breathe, she peered into his face. This close she could see that his eyes were the color of moonstones, but something in them made her stomach clench. She felt as if she should know him. There was something familiar about the bitterness in his eyes. But why? She'd never met anyone who looked like him.

The highlander took one last, long look at the portrait, and then crumpled it up as he walked back and tossed it into the fire. He never once glanced at Catriona.

While he stood with his back toward her she carefully crept away and returned to safety on the other side of the barrier. It had been beyond foolish to follow the man into the woods, and she should thank the gods that she'd escaped unscathed. She had to stop behaving so recklessly and do what she had come to the island to do.

Catriona walked back to the village, which had stood empty since her childhood. From its edge, she could spy the ocean and much of the land around. Though there were other places on the island she might stay, it was always to the village she returned. She spent every summer here planting new flowers, tidying up the cottages and visiting with the creatures that had taken shelter inside the barrier for the year. During the solstice she performed the remembrance ritual to honor her family, and pray for their return from the well of stars. Yet more than twenty years had passed since they'd died now. She came back every time hopeful that she would find Tavish and Isela waiting in new forms, her reborn parents ready to shower her with love again.

Mayhap the island is cursed, Catriona thought as she looked around the village.

Since the Moon Wake people had been slaughtered, not a single druid had ever come to live on Everbay.

Chapter Three

DEEP INSIDE THE basalt caverns of the Ninth Legion's subterranean stronghold on the Isle of Staffa, Quintus Seneca woke in darkness. Without thinking he reached for the woman of his dreams, the sweetly submissive lowland dairy maid who had enchanted him from the moment he had enthralled her. He would make love with Fenella Ivar as he drank from her veins, and begin his night with those two gratifying pleasures. Only when his cold hand touched empty linens did his folly disperse.

Fenella would never be with him anywhere but in his dreams.

Although she had died a year ago, her loss

remained an open wound. His poor love had died twice, in fact: once when Quintus had turned her undead after a lethal attack, and a second time during a battle with their immortal enemies, the McDonnel Clan. The fault for both of her deaths lay on him, and no weight he had ever carried in life had felt as crushing.

She had saved his life, and he had repaid her by sending her to her final death.

The door to his bed chamber opened, and a plump figure slipped inside. His second undead female creation, Bryn Mulligan, had brought a goblet of fresh blood. A former village whore who possessed none of Fenella's grace or beauty, she had still provided a welcome distraction these last months. Quintus had not turned her to serve as his new lover, but he sometimes still used her when his needs became pressing.

"Fair evening to you, Tribune." She stopped at a respectful distance and bobbed in a deep curtsey. "Prefect Strabo awaits you in the outer hall."

A veteran centurion, and one of the few

survivors of their last clash with the McDonnels, Titus Strabo had taken Fenella's place as
Quintus's prefect. He dutifully reported every
night on the progress he was making with
replacing the troops lost in battle. In most
ways he had become an acceptable second in
command, although he had little imagination,
and sometimes spoke with a surliness that
grated.

"Very well," Quintus said. He would not
hurry himself to attend to Strabo, whom he
resented for surviving when Fenella had
perished. "Bring that blood to me." When she
did he drained the goblet, and then inspected
her smiling face. "What have you to tell me of
your efforts, my dear?"

"Another ten female mortals have been
turned, milord." Bryn cast her gaze down with
her customary deference. "Once I have
instructed them, with your permission they
shall be placed to service the garrison."

He nodded, pleased that she sought his
approval for her plans. The women she was
teaching to work as whores would soon be
ready to leave Staffa and be placed where they

could enthrall large numbers of male mortals. Once enslaved the men would be used in various ways to protect and serve the Ninth. The strongest would be sent to Staffa to be turned and join the legion.

Quintus rose and dressed before he had Bryn fetch Strabo. His prefect presented himself in the hooded black cloak he'd worn over his uniform since being wounded. It billowed around him as he knelt and saluted with a forearm across his chest.

"Your vanity annoys me, Strabo."

"Apologies, Tribune." The prefect stood and tugged back the hood, revealing his scarred face.

Simply looking at the man further soured Quintus's mood. One half of Strabo's head still showed his weathered, rugged features, close-cropped hair and bullish neck as they had been. Burns from the battle had left the other side bald, darkened and twisted. Streaks of shiny scars extended around the blob that remained of his ear and disappeared under the edge of his chest plate. The contractions of his flesh as he'd healed pulled one side of his mouth up like an unending sneer.

Looking away from his prefect's ghastly visage would have been a sign of weakness, however, so Quintus kept his gaze steady on the unmarked half of his face. "What have you to report?"

Like every other night the news proved unremarkable. Strabo had dispersed the newest recruits to complete their training, and adjusted the ranks of two cohorts to accommodate them. Fresh thralls had been delivered by one of their black ships from the lowlands. No sign of the McDonnel clan had been seen by any of the scant patrols on the mainland.

"You must send more search teams to the highlands," Quintus told the prefect. "Have them begin at the ridges closest to the sea and work inland from there."

"Had I the men to spare, I would, Tribune," Strabo said, his ruined mouth struggling to shape some of the words. "The first cohort is barely a hundred men, and none with tracking experience. The second you sent to the lowlands to continue gathering blood thralls." He flicked his fingers at his scarred cheek. "I and two others are all that is left of the third, and the rest—"

"–have perished," Quintus finished for him. "As I am well aware, Prefect. Your training methods are proving too leisurely. Cut their blood rations to half, and double the drills."

Strabo's remaining brow arched above the narrow black crescent of his eye. "Tribune, to starve the newly-turned is to invite frenzy."

"Then post guards to protect the stronghold thralls, you idiot," Quintus snapped. "Or must I do your work as well as instruct you on how to manage it?"

"Not at all, my lord." Strabo bowed. "I shall see to it directly." He glanced at Bryn. "My lady."

Once the prefect departed Quintus regarded his whore mistress. "He shows more respect to you than me."

"He is bitter over his deformities," she said, startling him with the shrewd observation. "And I dinnae flinch away from him as the new mortal females do."

"Has he a bed slave?" When she shook her head, Quintus felt a little less annoyed. "Go to his chamber tonight and tend to him. Perhaps you can leech some of his ill temper before I lose mine and relieve him of his scorched head."

Bryn's cheeks plumped with her smile. "As you command, milord."

Chapter Four

AT DAWN CATRIONA rose from her pallet and wrapped her old wool blanket around her as she went to the hearth. She knelt down and fed some bits of wood to the banked embers until they woke and flared. Another pile of dried branches brought the flames to dance, and she smiled a little as she warmed her hands. The first time she'd tried to build a fire alone she'd scorched her fingertips and singed her hair. How terrified she'd been on that day, creeping about the island as if Uncle might jump out at her from behind every rock and tree.

Now Catriona had only to contend with a highlander who drew a beautiful woman, only to burn her portrait. That didn't frighten as much as unsettle her.

A chirp drew her attention to the mossy nest she had fashioned for the little nestling she'd rescued from a tidal pool. The bedraggled chick's minor wounds from tumbling out of its cliffside nest had healed, and now it was a plump ball of black fluff. Only when the end of its thin beak had begun to show a little orange did she know for certain that it was a baby puffin.

"Fair morning, Jester." She took down the bowl of fish and limpet mash she'd made last night, and came over to remove the woventwig basket that kept the bird from wandering off. As he caught some strands of her redbrown hair and tugged, she pinched a bit of the mash. With her fingers she placed it in the hungry chick's mouth in the same manner his mother might. "Och, you're a greedy thing. Dinnae gulp it so fast. Aye, that's the way of it."

Once she finished feeding the nestling she dressed in the warmth by the hearth. The cold nipped at her skin, making her think fondly of the thick robe she'd left at her

other home. She never brought any clothing
to the island except what she wore for traveling: a shawl Senga had knit for her, and a
gown Catriona had made by hand from old,
worn linen. She had many finer garments at
home, but she worried she might forget
something that would betray not only her
presence, but where she now lived away from
Everbay.

The one gown Catriona did leave behind
had belonged to her mother, and was her most
treasured possession. She could still remember
gathering woad leaves with Isela to dye the
kirtle and long skirts, but not the name of the
ritual for which her mother had made them.
Something about the light of the shore, and
the longest day. Losing her family before
growing old enough to enter the sacred circle
had left Catriona as ignorant as a newly-
weaned bairn. Ennis and Senga had sympa-
thized with her frustration, but they knew
nothing of the ways in which she should have
been trained.

"Senga isnae druid kind," Ennis admitted
when Catriona had spoken to him about her
lack of knowledge. "I've the blood but no' the

learning, nor the lives past to remember. As druids you and I are babes, lass."

Looking down at the faded, tattered linen she had clumsily repaired so many times, Catriona saw her life. She had been ripped apart, and each time she came back to the island she tried to heal, but something always tore her anew. By her second or third day she woke every morning sobbing, at least until the highlander had come. Catriona had always borne her sorrows alone, for she had never shared the island with another soul. Now each day she rose with anticipation instead of dread, eagerness instead of sorrow.

Wanting attention, Jester made a little clattering sound with its beak, and Catriona went over to sit with her hand over the chick until the warmth of her touch lulled it to sleep.

As she replaced the basket, she wished she had someone to comfort her. The pull the highlander had on her made her feel ashamed, especially for watching him from afar. Perhaps that was the only way she could love, from a distance, watching and wishing. It hurt to be so alone, but then she could never lose what she would never have.

Wrapping herself in Senga's warm blue shawl, Catriona left the cottage. From every other house in the village creatures watched her with bright, curious eyes. Their thoughts fluttered through hers in images, for they had no words. They all shared a kind of understanding of the world and living things, and recognized her as a friend, but not in the ways of people.

To the voles and hares, she was the gentle hand that fed them grain and roots, and offered them protection from the short-eared owls and sea eagles. To the eiders and gulls, she was a clever fisher and catch-sharer, to be followed whenever she went to the tidal pools. The island's shy deer liked her best when she ran with the herd up to the slopes. The goats still treated her like the odd, long-legged kid they had thought her as a wee lass. Even the enormous white swans, who came to the island during the winter only long enough to nest, grudgingly accepted her presence at the spring pool.

Catriona couldn't help but care for them all, for they were her only friends and teachers she'd ever had.

Today her feet took her beyond the village and out onto the glen, where she stopped to check the horizon. Storms came to the island with little warning, but Catriona sensed nothing brewing. The animals, whom the gods had attuned to the weather as she could never be, always warned her when she should stay indoors. The thud of an ax on wood caught her ear, and she turned to see a thin plume of white smoke coming from the forest.

The highlander never made a fire on the days he left the island. The smoke meant he would spend another night.

Watching the trees, Catriona moved to a darker spot before she crossed the barrier to enter the forest. The sounds of the ax ceased, and then came the pounding of a hammer. She moved silently through the dappled light, and tucked her arms around her waist to stop her hands from trembling. This was more than foolish, it was pure madness, and yet she could not stop herself from walking up to the edge of the clearing.

The highlander had fashioned a work table from some planked timbers and two old barrels. He plied his hammer against pegs,

driving them into bore holes on three-sided
rectangles of wood. Beyond the table lay on
the ground neatly-bundled thatching of reeds,
twigs and straw. Behind him the frame of the
cottage roof rose in golden peaks above the
finished walls.

The man stopped hammering and hefted
the thatch bundle, testing the sides before
adding it to a pile of others he'd finished. That
seemed to be the last, for he walked to the
cottage wall and hoisted himself up, balancing
on the double stone walls as he gripped a roof
beam at the base and tested it with a gentle
shake.

Dismay filled Catriona. He would finish
his cottage this very day, and she would never
be rid of him.

She felt the tug of him again, this time
in her chest, and abruptly turned her back
on the forest. Now he would come to live
in this house he built, and spend every
night here. When she came she would be
obliged to always remain on the other side
of the barrier, and that might not protect
her from discovery. Once the highlander
knew of her, he would talk to others.

More would come, and word would spread.

The druids had eyes and ears everywhere. Uncle would hear of her and come. He would come to silence her. If she wished to live, Catriona would have to leave the island for good, never to return.

From the forest Catriona followed a path that made her heart heavier with each step. It led to a smaller meadow on the other side of the glen. Wildflowers nodded their bright heads as she approached the broad oval of carved stones marking the place. The first time she had come alone to the island it had been winter. The swans, who of all the island's creatures had the longest memories, had accompanied her to the place where the tribe had been buried. They remembered the strange druids coming during their first nesting, and what the outsiders had done after finding the bodies.

Each time she came here Catriona still felt guilty.

She stopped just inside the stone oval, where gold and violet flowers grew in great profusion in the soft, sweet meadow grass. She knew the bodies in the ground were not the souls who had lived in the village, but only what had been left after they'd disincarnated.

"Our souls cannae die, sweetheart," her mother had told her after explaining why druids were not like mortals. "When we leave one body, we return to the well of stars. Then, when it is time for us to live again, we return to the mortal realm as newborns."

As not one of the Harals had ever returned to Everbay, Catriona suspected that they never would.

"I am here, and I think of you," she said as she sank down onto her knees, and pressed her hand to the warm earth. "'Twill be for the last time. I must go and stay with Ennis and Senga, and live my life with them. I will be safe."

We shall never be safe from the Vikings or the Romans, her uncle's silken voice whispered inside her head. *Only power will protect us.*

The conclave will never permit you to dabble in these magics, her father had told his brother flatly. *The people of the black land worshipped the dead.*

No, brother, they sought true immortality. We waste ourselves hopping from body to bairn. Uncle's eyes had glittered with a strange joy. *Once I possess all of the scrolls I will ken what must be done to set us free.*

Her father's expression grew hard. *I cannae permit it. You will abandon this notion, or I shall take you before the conclave myself.*

Uncle had bowed his head as he agreed, but Catriona had seen his eyes fill with malice. From that day he had grown distant and cold, openly avoiding Tavish and Isela, and frequently disappearing for days on end.

You must mend this rift with your brother, Isela had told her husband. *We cannae hold the summer celebration with such discord between you.*

I cannot conquer his fear, Tavish said, and sighed. *When he returns I shall speak with him again.*

Catriona had never learned what her uncle feared, but it had not been her parents. For them he had felt only contempt and hatred, and it showed in his ugly eyes every time he looked upon them without their seeing.

Time passed unnoticed as the sun warmed her shoulders, and a breeze from the slopes cooled her hot, wet face. Slowly Catriona rose

to her feet. As they ever did, thoughts of
Uncle had left her drenched in sweat. She
tugged at the damp linen of her kirtle, and
thought of the spring. The highlander would
be too busy working on his roof to intrude on
her there.

She returned to the village to collect her
traveling garments, some soap and a wrap for
her head. Senga would scold her if she
returned home with wet hair, Catriona
thought as she walked out to the spring.
Mortals had the oddest notions about sickness.
Druids rarely suffered illness. Even when she
was a wee lass, and the itching pox had
stricken nearly all the children of Ennis and
Senga's village, Catriona had not fallen sick.

This would be the last time she crossed the
barrier, Catriona thought as she stepped
through the spell wall and strode toward the
edge of the spring. After she bathed she would
take the nestling back to the cliffs, and then
use the sacred oak grove to make her journey
to the mainland. Ennis's birthday would come
in a few weeks, so she would have to think of
what she might–

The sound of a masculine sigh made

Catriona freeze in her tracks. Not a yard away from her lay the highlander, dripping wet and naked, stretched out on her sunning stone.

Her throat tightened, and she clutched her garments against her chest. How could he be here? Not half an hour past she had seen him preparing to thatch his roof. The slant of the sun answered her, for it was sinking toward the canopy of trees on the west side of the island. She must have sat for hours in the meadow and not realized it.

The highlander lay with his huge arms tucked under his head, his long bronze hair shedding water from his swim. His eyes were closed, and his chest rose and fell with the slowness of one dozing. If she made a single noise, he would look over and see her.

If he woke she could run for the barrier, through which he could not pass. She would pause only to take Jester from the cage. Left there, the nestling would starve.

She should run away, run now, this moment, but all she wanted was to look upon the man, and see all of his perfection —this once.

The highlander's position displayed in full

glory the thick length of his male member. Out of curiosity Catriona had taken two lovers since reaching womanhood, but neither of those eager lads could compare to this man. His long, vein-roped shaft should have seemed menacing, yet strangely she thought it as comely as the rest of him.

'Twill seem an unlikely business, Senga had said during a kind but blunt talk about sex. *'Tis best to trust your lad to see to it.*

The lads she'd trusted had both been sweet and gentle with her, and Catriona had enjoyed love-making. Yet how did a lass give herself to such a beast? Catriona eyed the highlander and imagined him naked and on top of her. She'd be squashed for certain, she thought, but the thought didn't make her shudder.

He had sunned himself without a tunic often enough to toast his smooth skin a golden brown from shoulders to belly. She remembered her father, who had been as tall as the highlander. Tavish had been fit but not half as wide nor padded with such powerful muscle. She could see in great detail the skinwork on the man's shoulder, which had been inked so finely the lion seemed ready to spring from his flesh and knock her to the ground. Truly she'd had no notion of how magnificent her intruder was. It made her feel the tug of him like a hard yank, one that could send her toppling upon him.

Catriona smiled a little. Would that not be the rudest of awakenings, to find a sweaty, blushing lass sprawled atop him?

The highlander breathed in deeply, and opened his eyes. They gleamed like silver crystals in the sunlight. "Fair day to you, Lady Ghost."

Catriona stumbled backward, turned and ran.

❦

GAVIN STAGGERED as he dragged on his trousers, but left behind his boots and tunic as he took off after the woman. The wild mane of chestnut hair whipped behind her, and he still saw the intense, violet-blue eyes wide with shock. She'd hiked up her skirts, showing long, curvy legs that ate up the ground in elegant strides. He grinned, pouring on the speed as the distance between them shrank. In another minute he'd catch her, and then he'd find out if she were real or wraith.

A moment later she vanished right in front of him, as if she had never existed.

Gavin stopped, frowning as he scanned the open glen from side to side. He couldn't see a single sign of where she'd gone. Yet he could still hear the light sound of her quick footsteps through the grass, growing fainter by the second. When he followed her trail through the grass the air took on a faint shimmer that engulfed him in a momentary tingling sensation. The glen around him bulged outward around him, as if he were stepping through a mirror, and then smoothed out.

On the other side of the looking glass was a very different glen, as if the one he'd been seeing for months didn't exist.

He looked for his wraith among the cluster of old cottages, but saw no sign of her. Everywhere he looked flowers and ivy sprouted, climbing the walls of the old structures, and splashing bits of color on the ancient thatching. The familiar perfume of the blooms mixed with the lighter scent of the greenery in the air. A light chinking sound drew his eyes to windchimes made of seashells strung on vines, which hung from the corners of every eave. Surrounding each cottage were dense beds of flowers, herbs and berry bushes. From them he spotted the flash of small, watchful dark eyes. As if on cue the two mated ducks who had visited him emerged from a burrow hole and waddled over to look up at him.

They were not the only ones watching. The back of his neck had that strange tension. He could sense her, somewhere close but hidden, staring out at him.

"I'll no' harm you, lass," Gavin said, holding out his arms so she might see his empty hands. "I've been told no one lived here, or I'd have come to call."

The male duck shook his head and nudged his female in the direction of their burrow.

"My name is Gavin, and I come from the highlands." He looked around until he spotted a worn stump and sat on it. "My crewmates have told me about you, but they think you a ghost." He waited for a reply, and when none came he added, "Your village is lovely. Did you plant all these flowers?"

A shuffling sound from inside the largest cottage gave Gavin her location, but he made no move to confront her. Instead he turned toward the open doorway and smiled.

"I finished the roof of my house today. I dinnae think the thatching will drop on my head while I'm sleeping, but I'd be glad to ken your opinion of it." He felt a bit like an idiot, talking in the utter silence. The stillness of the place didn't make sense to him. "Where are the rest of your people? I've no' seen anyone else here. Do you ken that they call you the Blue Lady of Marr?"

A brown hare crept out from beneath a thorny bramble bush, and hopped cautiously toward the male duck. Together they stood inspecting Gavin as if he had three heads.

"'Tis good that she looks after you." He was also glad he hadn't yet hunted anything on the island. It seemed the woman had made all of them her pets. "Do you reckon I can persuade her to talk to me, or should I leave now?"

A squawk came as a tiny ball of black down rushed out of the largest cottage. Gavin grinned as the nestling fluttered its stunted wings and puffed itself up, swelled as if trying to look bigger.

The duck and the hare exchanged an odd glance before they flanked the baby bird and tried to herd it back inside. The nestling darted between them, scurried over to Gavin and gave him a hard peck on the ankle.

The wee thing was actually attacking him.

"You've got spine, but I'm a bit more than you should be taking on." He leaned over and scooped up the nestling, which settled on his palm and regarded him steadily, as if trying to make up its mind whether to try another peck.

The scent of fish, along with the triangular patch of dark skin around the red-ringed black made Gavin guess it to be a baby puffin. He also spotted newly-healed scars on the chick's head and wing where pin feathers had begun to sprout.

"Your name must be Trouble," he told the nestling, and gently stroked its downy black head with a fingertip. The trilling sound it made in response felt like a compliment. Gently he placed the chick back on the ground, and watched it return to the cottage.

Gavin started seeing the village differently

now. The woman evidently rescued injured nestlings, and likely provided food and shelter for anything else in need. He'd kept a pair of finches for a time back home, as watching them calmed him and made his loneliness more bearable. Maybe she'd done the same, just on a larger scale.

That theory begged another question: Just how long had she been living alone here? Months, years? Back at the spring he'd gotten only a glance of her face, which had been flushed and filled with terror, but she was definitely young. He guessed she was in her twenties. Had she run away from her people? Why would she come to a place considered cursed? Was he the only other person she'd seen since coming to the island?

Gavin stood and walked over to one of the smaller cottages. He had to duck his head to enter through the open door, and once inside waited until his eyes adjusted to the shadowy interior.

Old cobwebs draped the corners of the large front room, and a thick layer of dust covered the simple handmade furnishings. On the table by the hearth lay empty wooden bowls and spoons. The cooking pot had been knocked from its hook and had landed on its side. A pile of twigs and fluff in the ashes of the fireplace suggested the chimney had become a regular nesting spot. From the amount and variety of animal tracks left on the dirt floor no human had lived here for years, possibly decades. Yet a fresh pine bough, decked with flowers, had been placed on the mantel, along with four white seashells.

Gavin walked back to the only other room, which had once been used as a bed chamber. Rotted linens lay in a tangle atop a frame of wood so old and weathered it sagged, ready to fall apart. An open trunk held mold-speckled clothing that had yellowed at every fold. A blackened wreath of what might have once been mistletoe hung over the remains of the bed.

Beneath the wreath a spray of rusty, patchy color stained the stone wall. It took Gavin another moment to realize that it was a very old blood stain.

He backed out of the door, and looked at the front room again. Now he could see more of the rusty stains on the walls and furnishings

and even in the dirt of the floor. They almost
screamed in the silence as he recalled what
Silje had told him about Marr.

*Dinnae jest about the Blue Lady of Marr. 'Tis
said she seeks vengeance for her tribe. They were
massacred by blood-drinkers.*

Could it be true? Gavin felt his skin crawl,
and hurried out of the cottage to stand in the
bright sunlight. Since coming to the islands, he
had put from his mind the nightmare of the
undead. If Silje's story were real then this
woman lived surrounded by constant
reminders of what they had done to the
people here.

Why would she choose to live in such a
place? Why had she planted flowers and
festooned the decaying remains of a ghost
village? It was like decorating a grave.

Gavin went to stand in the center of the
settlement, and counted the cottages. There
were twenty-seven of them, and if each had
held a family, that meant hundreds had died
here. If she had some connection to the lost
tribe, perhaps it was some kind of memorial.

"I ken that the people here suffered," he
said, keeping his tone soft. "Blood-drinkers are

terrible creatures that kill without thought or care. They are so fast and strong that naught can escape them, and they are merciless with their victims." He turned his head and touched the scars Thora had left on the side of his neck. "I was used by one who enslaved me. In the end I escaped, but I lost everyone I loved."

Animals began coming out of the cottages and flower beds, and for a moment Gavin wondered if they would attack him. But while they watched him with unblinking eyes, none of them appeared to be hostile, or afraid. He crouched down as a trio of small hares crept close, and offered his hand for them to sniff.

"I journeyed to the islands to start a new life," he said as he gave the boldest leveret a gentle scratching behind its small ears. "I built my house here because I'm no' yet ready to be around other people. I thought if I lived alone, I might heal and find some peace in myself. That hasnae happened, but I still hope 'twill."

He straightened and looked at the largest cottage, and thought he saw a flutter of blue move across the doorway—and there was that familiar scent.

"I've intruded long enough, my lady. I promise, I willnae bother you again." Gavin smiled down at the animals gathered around him. "I'm leaving for work in two days, but I will return each night. You ken where to find me." He hesitated before he added, "Unless you'd like to come out and meet me now."

⚜

CATRIONA BACKED away from the window, and whirled around to hurry into her bed chamber. She had already packed most of her things. She needed only to assure she'd left nothing behind that would show she yet lived. The highlander could not have gotten a good look at her. He would remember only the blue dress.

Maybe if Uncle heard of that, he would think the island haunted by her mother. That would please Catriona enormously.

The animals she had sent to inspect the man plagued her with images of his smile, and the gentle touch of his hand. The ducks liked his voice, and the hares considered him trustworthy enough to let him fondle their leverets. Even Jester, now safely stowed under the basket, chittered to be let out again to see the highlander.

She felt like shrieking with frustration. His kindness had to be false—a ruse, to draw her out into the open. He wanted her to think him harmless so she would be careless, and put herself at his mercy. Her uncle had been exactly the same.

No, he hadn't. Catriona sat down on the edge of her bed and buried her face in her hands. Uncle had smiled and spoken and even jested, but the ice in his eyes had never thawed. He'd often patted her on the head, as if she were a family pet and not a child. Each time the touch of his soft hand had made her stomach surge into her throat.

The highlander had no idea who she was or why she had come here, and she would keep it so. Catriona shoved her garments in her satchel and slung it over her shoulder. As soon as she collected herself, she would go out through the back door of the cottage, and weave her way through the others until she was safely out of sight. Then she could reach

the sacred grove, and use the portal to return
to Ennis and Senga.

She would never come to Everbay again.

Catriona went to the window to take one
last look at the highlander. He stood waiting,
his hands at his sides, his expression one of
patience and understanding. He knew nothing
of her, and yet there he remained, with his
bare chest and feet, his hair a damp tangle,
and the sunlight turning his eyes to
warm amber.

He looked like everything kind, and yet he
had burned the sketch of the woman. Was she
one he had lost? Or was that another lie?

Something about him felt wrong, but
something more felt right. The more Catriona
looked upon him, the more she felt the pull of
him, the goodness of him. He worked hard,
he showed kindness to her friends, and he
apologized for trespassing. Perhaps everything
he said was the truth.

What did she truly know of him, except
that he had crossed the barrier?

In that moment she knew why he had such
an aura of goodness. Her knees wobbled as
she turned away from the window, and she

pressed her hand over her burning eyes for a moment as the realization cut through her. Mortals could not pass through the spell wall. She knew that from the few times others had tried. Her barrier had failed to keep Gavin away, and there was only one reason for that.

Somehow, impossibly, he was druid kind.

That was what had drawn her to him. Ennis had had the same effect on her the first time they'd met. Gavin shared the same blood as she had. He also might know more about Druidry than Ennis had. She would never know unless she went out there and spoke to him.

Catriona looked down at herself. Every part of her trembled with fear, and her breath rushed in and out through her nose and mouth. Since the attack she had kept from everyone in the islands. If she were to go outside and face him, first she had to calm herself. She pulled Senga's shawl from her satchel, wrapping it around herself. The feel of the soft wool soothed her enough to stop her shaking. She had only to get close enough to him to feel his life energy, and then she would know.

All around the village the animals went still as she reached out to them with her thoughts one last time. She trusted their senses more than her own, and from what they thought back to her they believed she would be safe with the man.

Catriona took a deep breath, and marched out of the cottage. She stopped short of the highlander by several yards, and prepared to run if need be.

"My name is Catriona. I suppose that I am the Blue Lady they speak of, but this island is called Everbay, no' Marr."

The breeze whisked away the sound of her voice, leaving them in a palpable silence. Gavin stared at her as if aghast, his brow furrowed and his mouth shaped a word without sound.

Why did he gape at her like that? Had he never before seen a woman? As his gaze traveled over her, she took a step back. While she would never be the beauty Isela had been, she knew herself to be comely and well-shaped. Perhaps he found fault with her mother's precious gown. To him it must seem like a bundle of rags.

"Well? Have you naught to say to my face?" she demanded.

That broke his trance. "Forgive me, I… 'Tis a pleasure to meet you, my lady." He peered at her again. "You *are* real."

"Aye, as you see." She must have given him a fright at the spring, and felt a little ashamed for speaking so gruffly to him. "I wear blue, but I am no' a lady."

"Mistress Catriona, then." He glanced down at the leverets, two of which now perched on his feet. "I thought the name of this island to be Marr."

"'Tis what mortals call it now." Catriona jerked her chin at his skinwork. "I have never seen the like of your ink. Where does your tribe call home?"

Some of the ease left his features. "I have no tribe."

That explained why he had come to the island alone. "Nor do I."

Gavin's mouth curled on one side. "The people on the other islands believe you to be a ghost."

"Mayhap I am." She didn't want to like him, but already his attention had softened her. He had a way of looking at her that made her feel bonny, even in the shreds of her mother's gown. *What he thinks of me matters no'*, she reminded herself. "What shall you tell them now?"

Gavin looked around the village. "You've been hiding from me all this time. You mustnae wish anyone to learn of you."

Now she might say too much, and he would tell others. "I dinnae live here. I but visit this place now and then. I will go, and leave the island to you."

"You neednae do that." He took a step toward her, and then stopped when he saw her reaction. "Mistress, I meant what I said. Please, dinnae leave. I willnae harm you."

Catriona had no ear for truth or lies, but her friends did. The hares eyed her as they thought of how gentle he treated their leverets, and Jester after the nestling's clumsy attack. They too had warmed to him, and they were not easily deceived. "Why would you wish me to stay?"

"I came here from the mainland, and still have much to learn about island living." He gestured around them. "And I can see that you have spent much time here. It must feel like your home."

Too much. Catriona thought of Ennis and Senga, whom she loved, and the quiet little hamlet where she lived with them. She loved them both. They had generously provided her with sanctuary and comfort away from Everbay, but the highlander was right. Only when she came back to the island did she feel at home.

That he knew nothing of the islands and yet had chosen to build his cottage on Everbay puzzled her. "Why do you come to dwell here? Wouldnae you be happier in the highlands?"

His eyes darkened, and he glanced back at the cottage behind him. "I left behind too many unhappy memories to do that."

"You cannae escape," Catriona said without thinking, and hunched her shoulders. "We carry them with us."

"Aye, but 'tis my hope they fade in time." He looked all over her face. "How long do you stay for your visit?"

Her suspicions sent spikes of fear through her. Did he have some scheme to work on her? Had Uncle sent him to hunt for her? Who might have betrayed her presence? As her thoughts snarled, she forced herself to meet his gaze. "Why do you care?"

"Down by the shore there are some shell-fish I've never before seen," Gavin said, and pointed in the direction of the cove of tidal pools. "I dinnae ken if they are safe to eat. Will you come with me there, so I may show you?"

Catriona started to refuse, and then thought better of it. The man had to eat, and anything he took from the sea would keep him from hunting her friends. In the water there were plenty of scallops, clams and mussels to be had, but there were other cautions to take. As a highlander used to fresh water lochs he likely did not know the dangers.

"I will walk with you," she said at last, but she let him lead and kept her distance.

They stopped first at the spring, where the highlander retrieved his garments and boots. Catriona turned away as he dressed, trying to think of something to say in the interval. She had never had to speak to anyone on the island before now, and back in the village and at work she avoided talking because her brogue was so different and heavy.

"I'm fit to be seen now," he announced.

That was the problem. All she wanted to do was look at him. "I see you bringing fish with you when you come from the ferry." And now he knew she had watched him, Catriona thought, cringing a little. "Do you work on the docks, or a boat?"

As they crossed the glen, Gavin spoke of the fisher out of Hrossey harbor on which he crewed. The cod he sometimes brought to the island came from the cold waters of the North Sea, which Catriona knew to be rich but often dangerous.

"My share of the catch is always more than I can eat, so I give what I cannae use to the men with families," Gavin said. "Soon I reckon I should smoke or dry some for the cold months."

"'Tis easier to salt," she said, and nodded at the thick deposits of silver-white sea salt on the rocks hemming the shore. "You layer fish and salt in a crock or barrel, and leave it for a day to draw out the liquid. Then repack all in fresh salt, and 'twill keep for three seasons."

She saw the way he looked at her and shrugged. "I eat fish. So many fill the seas they can never be counted. They dinnae feel things as furred and feathered creatures do."

"I thought mayhap you lived on rose petals and morning dew," he said gravely.

Was he teasing her now? Catriona scowled to keep her lips from curving. "Show me your strange shellfish."

Gavin led her down to a wide rock pool filled with oysters, anemones and other colorful shellfish. He crouched down and pointed to a colony of long, narrow gray shells with long brown fringes. Even from several paces back she could easily see through the perfectly clear water.

"What do you call these, Mistress?"

"Sandies," she said, using the islander name for mussels. "They are good steamed with wild garlic. You can take them from this pool, but the largest shall be full of grit, and the smallest have no taste." She glanced at his face. "Take only those that are middling, shorter than your thumb." With her fingers she measured the proper size in the air.

He nodded. "But why from this pool and no' another?"

Catriona led him over to a smaller pool with blue-green blooms floating around the edges. "See the scum there?" Though he came closer for a good look, she didn't back up this time. "'Tis a sun blight. It grows where the water is too still and warm, and taints everything around it. Always look for it first. Eat from a scummed pool, and if it doesnae kill you, 'twill put you on your back to puke in your bed for sevenday or longer."

He watched her as she returned to the clean pool, reached into the water and deftly scooped up a spiky green sea urchin. As soon as he saw what she held he made as if to step toward her but stopped himself.

"'Tis a dangerous thing to hold," he said.

"If I clutch it too tightly, aye. You've only to treat it as you may a hedgehog, with care." She took a few steps back toward him and gently rolled over the spiny ball to show him the toothy mouth circle. "You open it here, with a blade run along the outside of the teeth. Break off the spikes first so you may grip the shell as you cut, and dig out the five orange parts inside to eat."

"Raw?" When she nodded Gavin winced. "I reckon I'll stay with steaming the middling sandies."

"And you a fisherman," Catriona said and placed the urchin back in the pool. "Watch for green urchins wherever you take your shellfish. Where you see them in abundance, there willnae be blight in the pool."

"Because they eat it," he guessed.

"Aye." She suspected he was clever enough to learn on his own how to survive here, but it would do no harm to show him how to fish in her waters. "Has your crew taught you how and where to net from the shore?"

Gavin had only fished from a boat deck, so she showed him the recess up in the rocks where she kept her oak-bast nets. One of the loom weights she'd tied to the corners fell on the sand, and she quickly restrung it before leading him into the shallows.

"When you see nothing in the water you must spread bait, like so," Catriona told him, gesturing with her hand. "Chop some snails or worms to attract the most." A bright cluster of fish swimming toward them flashed under the water. "There, now. We call those silver darlings, for they are fat and savory."

Catriona waited patiently as the school of herring approached, and when they swarmed around them she cast her net. Most of the fish evaded it, turned and fled for deeper waters. But a dozen wriggled madly as they tried in vain to find a way out.

"You tuck the far end under and draw it toward you," she told him as she pulled the net closed, and hefted it out of the water. "Cinch the weights together, and you have your catch."

"Do you want them?" Gavin asked, and when she shook her head he took the net from her, their hands brushing briefly. A strange tingle shot up her arm, and for his part the Highlander stared at where she'd touched him. But after the briefest pause, he tossed two of the fish onto the shore before releasing the rest under water. "I've my firesteel in my pocket, and I'm hungry. What say we build a fire and cook those fish?"

She hadn't shared a meal on the island with anyone since her parents had died, and started to refuse. Then she looked into his eyes, and saw her own loneliness reflected there. He didn't want her to leave him, and there was pleasure in knowing that.

"Aye, Highlander," she said. "I'll gather the wood."

Chapter Five

O NCE THE SUN set, Strabo regarded the men standing in perfect ranks on the grass cliff top. Only one in every ten were true Romans who had come to this land with him twelve centuries past. Now the legion had become rife with the likes of Norse raiders and peasant farm hands and Nubian slaves. Most could not read or cipher, and they had to be forced to bathe. Dozens of female thralls had died beneath them, for they rutted like animals without the least care for what damage they inflicted.

Still, they were his men, and train them he would.

"Look upon me," he shouted as he pulled

back his hood. "This is the best that you may expect from the highlanders. The worst will leave you as ash on the wind. You will repeat all of the fighting drills tonight and every night hence until you can perform them without mistake. These are your tribune's orders."

None of the men made a sound in response to his announcement, but many eyes narrowed and hands knotted.

"Run them again," Strabo told his centurions before he turned and strode back to the steep shelf of stairs hewn into the cliffside.

Guards came to attention as he passed them on the way to his chamber, and Strabo nodded to each man. For months he had been cultivating the troops' loyalty, which he now considered his most important weapon. Soon he felt certain the men would follow him into the bowels of the underworld without hesitation.

He had no fear of death. He wore it like a half-mask now, as if every day of his immortality would be a dark Saturnalia, and he a caricature of the two-faced god, Janus.

As soon as Strabo stepped inside his chamber he smelled the sweetness of honey.

Adorning his spartan furnishings were vases filled with bunches of the tiny, fragrant white flowers that festooned the cliffs. Beside his hearth sat Bryn Mulligan, her soft white body wrapped in the scantiest of black furs.

"Fair evening, Prefect Strabo." As she rose she allowed her generous breasts to spill out of the fur. "I am sent to tend to you."

"Indeed." She would not have come to him on her own, but at least she did not avert her eyes like the other females. "I have no need of you or your gifts." He gestured at the flowers. "Take these away."

Bryn pouted. "I thought to brighten your dreary rooms." She sidled up to him, her pale flesh gleaming in the firelight. "'Tis naught but a bit of pleasure, milord. How long has it been since you enjoyed a woman?"

"That is not your concern."

"I ken you dinnae pleasure yourself." She held up between them the sacred phallus from his private altar to Priapus. "This I found covered in dust."

The sacrilege would have outraged him, but Strabo knew she'd desecrated his shrine deliberately, as she did everything else.

"When I want a woman, I will take one."
He thrust her away. "Get out or I will summon
the guard."

"That will no' please the Tribune. He
thinks you sullen and petulant for lack of pleasure." Bryn wandered over to his bed. "I have
made sure of that."

"What?" Strabo peered at her. "Why?"

"To protect you. 'Tis Quintus Seneca and
his lack of regard for the legion that sticks in
your craw." She turned and sat down on the
edge of his bed. "He's the reason most of your
men are dead, and you maimed."

For a moment he wondered if the tribune
had sent his whore mistress to trap him into a
confession. "I should kill you right now."

"Then you would never learn what I ken,"
she chided. "'Tis more than you think, Titus.
The tribune grieves for the loss of that stupit
cow, Fenella Ivar. Your presence, aye, your
very face reminds him that he did naught to
protect her, his poor love."

Fascinated now, Strabo came to stand over
her. "What more have you to tell me?"

"Much." Bryn's placid eyes glittered. "I

despise Quintus Seneca as much as you. Give me what I desire, and I'll help you end him."

He could put her to death simply for confessing her hatred of the tribune, and she knew it. "What do you want?"

Bryn lay back on his bed, and parted her naked thighs. "Fack me now, and I'll tell you."

Chapter Six

NOW THAT IT was night, Gavin spread his jacket on the sand beside the fire they'd built by the rocks, and invited his new neighbor to share it.

"My skirts are still damp," Catriona said, and then shivered visibly as the chilly breeze swept over her. "Mayhap 'twill help them dry."

He nodded, and dropped more dried driftwood onto the flames before he settled down beside her. Tending the fire kept him from staring at her face, which already haunted him like some cursed cameo. She had delicate features, just sensual enough to avoid looking girlish, with velvety dark red brows and matching eyelashes framing her tanzanite eyes.

The color of her skin was one shade more golden than alabaster, and translucent enough to show the blue of her veins like shadows of dark lace.

For some reason he couldn't fathom, she was familiar—and yet not. Her fragrant scent cast his mind to the future. Had he perhaps known a descendant of hers? Or perhaps a relative on the mainland?

"You have left the island, Highlander," Catriona said, giving him a gentle nudge with her elbow—which he noticed but tried to ignore. "Where do you go in your head?"

Should he tell her that in seven hundred years she might have a lovely descendent? If he did that, he would have to admit to being a time traveler, dropped into the past by some force that had also healed him of an incurable disease.

She would think he was insane. He sometimes wondered himself if he was.

"You dinnae have to tell me," Catriona said. "Oft times the past is too painful for words."

"I was thinking about my parents' place." That had been a poor choice of lies, he thought. Although it had been years now, Gavin still hated that his sister had been forced to sell their family home to pay his medical bills. "We lived in a country farmhouse. No' grand at all, but a happy place for a lad to grow up."

"Away from here, I live in a small village." She plucked a bit of dried kelp from her skirt and flicked it into the flames. "'Tis quiet, but the people are kind and caring." Her mouth thinned. "If no' for my family... I'm most fortunate."

She didn't want to offer many details of her life away from the island, Gavin suspected, and wondered why she feared being more specific.

"I'll no' tell anyone what you confide in me, Mistress."

"Catriona," she said, giving him a wry look. "No fine lady would ken how to fish, or share such a meal, or sit on your coat. Besides those things, I've seen you naked."

"There is that." He chuckled. "Agreed, if you will call me Gavin, or Highlander, if you prefer."

"You're no' in the highlands anymore, lad,

but you're no' yet an islander. Gavin 'twill be."
She looked out at the dusky purple horizon. "I
never tire of being here. Sometimes I've
thought of coming back to stay. The winters
are no' so harsh. There's snow, but no' the
great storms that bury you in it."

As she talked about the seasons on the
island Gavin gradually realized her knowledge
could not have come from spending a few days
visiting now and then, as she had claimed.
When she fell silent he asked, "How long have
you been coming here by yourself?"

Catriona cocked her head and thought
about it. "'Tis twenty years now. I come for
some days when I dinnae have work, or when
my family is away. Sometimes I stay a week or
two, when the weather is fair."

Gavin had never seen her on the ferry, but
if she lived on one of the smaller islands to the
west she could row herself across the channel.
"Do you ever bring your family with you?"

"No. They ken 'tis my place, and I would
never…ask it of them." Her shoulders shook,
and she wrapped the shawl tighter around
herself. "The fire wants more wood."

If they hadn't been sitting on his jacket

Gavin would have given it to her. Instead he extended an arm to her. "Come closer. I've enough heat for us both."

"'Tis no' seemly," she pointed out, but her teeth chattered on the final word. Her face grew stern as she focused on the space between them. Finally she met his gaze. "Just for warmth, naught more."

"Naught more," Gavin echoed as she scooted closer, and he wrapped his arm around her.

At first Catriona felt like a bundle of kindling against his side, but gradually she relaxed and snuggled closer. The wind caught her hair and wrapped it around the back of his neck like a fragile scarf of copper and bronze silk. The scent of the sea came from her drying skirts, but beneath it he caught a trace of something soft and green, the way the ferns in the glen smelled when they first sprouted. This close he could see the calluses on her hands—only wealthy women in this time had soft, pampered skin—but the ovals of her fingernails were trimmed and clean.

It seemed impossible that this ethereal creature had been rowing herself back and forth to the island for the last twenty years. Still, Gavin knew even the children of this time were much tougher and self-reliant than their counterparts in the future. They had to be. Silje had told him that his oldest son would be joining the crew as a deck hand next year at the ripe old age of eight.

He heard a low purr, and looked down to see Catriona had fallen asleep. Her face looked much younger in repose, as if sleep smoothed away her years and returned her to the little girl she'd been.

Twenty years coming alone to this island inhabited only by a ghost village. Just to think of how alone she must have felt made his heart clench.

Gavin settled back against the rock, and gently lifted her onto his lap. She stirred briefly before slumping across his chest and tucking her face under his chin. Catriona likely would never have come so close to him awake, so he felt a twinge of guilt. Holding her in his arms while she slept, however, was the best feeling he'd had since coming to the islands.

Stars twinkled blue-white against the dark

navy sky as the wind settled and the waves lapped the shore. Gavin couldn't remember ever feeling more at peace than he did in this moment, holding his elusive new friend. Everything that had preyed on him had dimmed. The pain from his disease, the terror of losing his sister, the fear of being hunted or killed. It was as if the universe had decided to make his life a clean slate, on which he could write whatever he wanted.

Catriona. Gently he stroked his big hand over her long hair. Hers was the first name he wanted to write on his new life's slate, but he'd not yet erased the old one. The night was growing colder, and even his profuse body heat wouldn't keep her comfortable for much longer. He needed to see her safely home.

"Time to wake, lass," he murmured, rubbing her back.

"Hmmm." She shifted against him, lifting her head to meet his gaze with a drowsy smile. "You make a fine bed, Gavin."

The sexy huskiness of her voice whispered with her breath on his mouth, and hot desire rushed through him. "You make my thoughts turn unseemly, my lady."

He bent his head to kiss her brow just as she straightened, and their mouths brushed. For a moment she went still, and then curled her hand around his neck.

"Again, please." When he didn't move she smiled. "I'm no' a lady, Gavin. If you're to kiss me, do it proper."

That was all the permission he needed. Gathering her to him, he tilted her so that her head lay in the crook of his arm, and put his mouth to hers. She made that slumberous purring sound, like a beguiled feline, and parted her soft lips for him. Gavin cupped her jaw as he tasted her, her skin like satin against his rough fingers. The very air around them seemed to fill with some strange, unseen energy. Maybe it came from her, for she went to his head like chugged whiskey, her scent filling his chest with their mingled moans of pleasure. He could hold her and kiss her like this until the sun rose, until winter came, until time ended. She felt it, too, her willowy body pressing against him as if she wanted no space between them.

No woman had ever kissed him with such frank, sensual honesty. Not even Thora—

Gavin took his mouth from Catriona's, and eased her back. "I forget myself. 'Tis been a long time since I've held a woman. Forgive me."

She stared at him, her breath rushing from her parted lips, and then she touched his mouth with trembling fingers. "We share blood."

Had he hurt her? No, he could see that her mouth, still damp from his, didn't have a mark on it. "I dinnae understand your meaning."

"You are druid kind, Gavin." She took his hand in hers, and he felt the shimmering sensation again. "As I am. Seeing you from afar, I thought mayhap you were, but now I feel it. 'Tis how you were able to come through the spell barrier around the village. Only a druid may." Anticipation lit up her face. "I've never learned the old ways. Would you teach me what you ken?"

Gavin had seen enough magic since crossing over not to doubt her sincerity. He also hated to disappoint her, but all he knew how to do was use his own strange gift, which would be useless to her. "I've learned naught about druids or their ways. I was, ah, raised by others."

"Aye, the same for me." Her shoulders slumped as she released his hand. "'Twas foolish to hope."

The despair in her voice cut through him like a dull blade. He'd felt the same after Thora's betrayal of his love, and Jema's relief in thinking he was dead.

"'Tis growing cold." He stood, drawing her to her feet as he did, and bent to retrieve his jacket. After shaking the sand from it, he draped it over her narrow shoulders. "Come, now. I'll walk you home."

Catriona hardly spoke as they made their way to the glen. Once they reached the spell barrier, she didn't release his hand, but made as if to lead him through it.

"I'll say fair night to you here," Gavin told her.

She gave him an odd look. "Are you done with me then, Highlander?"

"'Twould please me to have you as my first guest at the cottage." He nodded toward the forest. "Come tomorrow at sunset, and I'll cook for you. 'Twill no' be duck or hare."

"My thanks." Quickly she stood on tiptoe to brush her lips across his cheek. "Tomorrow, then."

Her shawl fluttered as she stepped through the barrier, and vanished from sight. Gavin stood listening as the sound of her footsteps retreated, and touched his face where it still tingled.

Chapter Seven

CAILEAN LUSK'S ROBE swirled around his boots as he climbed the slopes above the druid settlement. After having his evening meditation disrupted by yet another spell ripple, he knew he had no choice but to disturb his master. Bhaltair Flen would not be pleased, but if what he suspected was true, more than the old druid's ire would descend on him.

The questions that plagued him all distilled into one: How could it be happening, after all this time?

The altar to which Bhaltair tended had been dedicated to the Great Mother, with two overlapping circles of carved stone forming a third pointed-oval center. Standing in the center invited the pleasure of the gods to provide the path of decision, which his master had been consulting regularly as to the fate of their Great Design. Thus far the gods had been silent, but Bhaltair remained optimistic.

As Cailean approached the altar clearing he politely coughed to announce himself, and then waited at the edge of the outer boundary for his master. Moonlight cloaked the old druid and the aura of his spell work, which appeared like a curtain of crystal. The casting encircled him for a moment before it floated to the ground and sank into the soil.

With an audible sigh Bhaltair knelt in gratitude before he left the center and walked toward Cailean. "The gods dinnae reveal their purpose—again. Either I have displeased them, or they are no' yet ready to enlighten me. Mayhap both." His sharp dark eyes shifted as he inspected Cailean's face. "You are looking wan. Never tell me another female from the future has arrived. We shall be overrun."

"Not as yet, Master." He belatedly remembered to bow. "I seek your guidance with an old matter, from my last incarnation."

Bhaltair's brows drew together. "'Tis been twenty years since you transcended." His gaze searched Cailean's face. "Naught to do with Everbay."

"Aye, I fear 'tis, Master." Cailean folded his chilled hands into the ends of his sleeves. "May we walk?"

The old druid accompanied him from the sacred ground along a trail that led to the small loch near the settlement. A flock of their sheep grazed near the water's edge, where the soft grass grew in abundance. Cailean drew comfort and calm from the bucolic sight, for just the opposite crowded his thoughts.

Bhaltair stopped and sat on a flat-topped rock, groaning a little as he rolled his stiff shoulders. "My knees willnae propel me another step. Best tell me, lad."

"Just before the end of my previous life, the conclave sent me to Everbay, to perform the last honors for the Moon Wake people." He reached down as a small ewe wandered over to him, and scratched the dense wool around her floppy ears. "'Twas just after we had word that the undead attacked their island, and killed all but one of the Harals."

"I remember. When Daimh Haral returned from his journey to Francia, he grew so distressed we thought he might disincarnate to join them." The old druid planted his gnarled hands on his knees as he leaned forward. "'Twas a painful task, I imagine."

"Honoring the dead by burying them is never a joy, but we did more than put the bodies in the ground. The tribe had unusual powers, and their village remained a hub of such. The conclave felt it could be dangerous to unknowing mortals." He made a circling gesture. "We cast a spell barrier around it to protect the place. I then directed our mortal allies in the islands to spread word that Everbay was forever haunted by the spirits of those massacred."

Bhaltair nodded his approval. "A sensible solution. When did the conclave send you to dismantle the village?"

"They didnae." As his master's jaw dropped Cailean grimaced. "'Twas the conclave's aim to resettle Everbay again someday when the Harals were reborn. The barrier was left intact to guard the village until that day came. The tribe hasnae returned to us yet. Daimh didnae take a wife to continue the bloodline, so he remains the last Haral."

"A deserted druid settlement left intact. Gods protect us." The old druid dragged his hand over his halo of silver hair. "What more?"

"I've been feeling the spellwork left there ripple many times over the last weeks," he admitted. "Since it cannot be breeched by anyone but druid kind…"

"'Tis a sacred grove on this island?" When Cailean nodded his master groaned and stood. "We must see what conspires there."

Cailean accompanied Bhaltair to his home, where they both washed and changed into fresh robes before entering the old druid's spell chamber. The room appeared empty until the door closed, and the protective wards dispersed. In the center of a spell circle stood a flat-topped stele of petrified wood. Beyond it on the wall, shelves held various focal stones and crystals which Bhaltair used when casting. He went to retrieve a large, pointed agate with a starburst of multi-colored striations framing a long, convoluted heart of purple and bronze crystals. Cailean recognized it as a window stone. The interior crystals glowed softly in response to the old druid's touch.

"I havenae attempted such a viewing, Master," Cailean felt he had to confess. "'Tis no' permitted at my level, and said to be fraught with hazard."

"Aye, for that is what we tell you ovates, to keep you from tampering with old enchantments." Bhaltair placed the window stone atop the stele. "Join hands with me. You will need my power meshed with yours for the stone to make such a reach."

Casting off his qualms, Cailean gently clasped the old druid's fingers from the other side of the crystal, forming an oval around it with their arms.

"Open your thoughts and see the place as 'twas at the time you cast the barrier spell," Bhaltair murmured as he joined his magic to Cailean's. The sphere took on a brighter luminescence before it turned a vivid sky-blue and showed waves crashing onto a rugged cliffside shore. "Everbay?"

Cailean nodded. "The Moon Wake tribe

dwelled in the glen in the center of the island."

The image shown by the crystal shifted to that of a lush grassy stretch of land wrapped around a small spring. A long wall of reflective enchantment stretched across the glen, dividing it almost in half.

Bhaltair scowled. "You mirrored the whole of the glen?"

"At the time 'twas the most enduring enchantment within my means, Master. The islanders were convinced to fear the place." He felt the knot in his belly tighten another notch. "The Moon Wake were a strong, healthy tribe with many bairns. After burying them all, I never wished to return to Everbay. I deliberately put it from my thoughts. I was happy the next winter, when my old body finally wore out. I thought I wouldnae dream of them again when I reincarnated."

"We cannae escape our memories, even in death and rebirth." The old druid's expression softened. "Dinnae torment yourself, lad. You shouldnae have been given such a responsibility. Still, we may attend to it now together. Recall now the first ripple you felt."

Reaching into the part of his mind closely connected with his magic, Cailean summoned the sense of the disruption, and projected it to the stone. The sun rose in the west as time reversed, and a large, bare-chested male stepped out of the barrier. The ink work on his shoulder showed a lion rampant against crossed bars. The male ran backward as another figure, a smaller, slender female in a torn blue gown, also emerged.

Cailean watched as the crystal replayed the scene again as it had happened in real time, with the male chasing after the female. He did not recognize either of them, but the ink on the male's shoulder had already been described to him.

"They are both druid kind," Bhaltair said, "but it appears that the male caused the magic to flux." He released Cailean's hands and the images from the glen vanished. "Why do you look as if I've kicked you in your smalls?"

"I think that male is Gavin McShane." He brought his hand to his brow to wipe away the cold sweat gathered there. "Brother to Jema, Tormod Liefson's wife."

"Gavin McShane, the twin brother killed

during the battle over Freyja's Eye?" Bhaltair sounded incredulous

"Aye, Master. I never met the man, but Mistress Liefson gave his description when we searched for his body." Cailean touched his own shoulder. "The skinwork of the lion and the bars looks to be the same."

"How does a man dead a year cross a barrier on an island twenty leagues from where he drowned?" Before he could reply the old druid made a dismissive gesture. "We cannae yet assume 'tis McShane. We must travel to Everbay to see the man in person. Before that, we must consult with Lachlan McDonnel on the matter." He removed the window stone from the stele and replaced it on its shelf. "We shall use the grove to travel to Skye directly and speak with the laird this night. Come, Ovate."

Cailean knew why his master was taking the matter to the McDonnel laird instead of Jema Liefson. After crossing over from the future, Gavin McShane had been enthralled by the Ninth Legion Prefect, Fenella Ivar. Fenella had then been possessed by Thora the Merciless, who had used Gavin and the undead in an attempt to kill the McDonnels with Freyja's Eye. Just as Thora's undead body had been destroyed by the ancient Norse relic, the release of power had hurtled Gavin into the sea. His body had never been found, so it had been assumed that it had been swept out to sea by the currents.

If Jema's brother hadn't died during the battle, then why hadn't he shown himself? Did he, too, possess the gift of invisibility, as his sister did? Twin siblings sometimes did. But why would he be on Everbay chasing after a female? Had he fallen under the sway of the undead again? And who was this druidess? Had she become somehow trapped on the island?

Cailean kept silent as he journeyed with Bhaltair through the sacred oak grove portal near their settlement. Emerging from another grove located near the Black Cuillin mountains on the Isle of Skye, he waited for his master to join him and then began the long walk into the ridges, where Dun Aran, the McDonnel Clan's stronghold, lay hidden.

The night wind chilled Cailean, but he hardly felt it as every step seemed to add new weight on his shoulders. If he had properly attended to the Moon Wake tribe's empty village, Gavin McShane would not present such a threat. The very real prospect of an untrained druid having access to the kind of power still contained on Everbay made him feel sick.

Climbing the trail through the ridges left Bhaltair short of breath, and Cailean had to shake off his worry as they approached the castle.

"We have come to speak with the laird on an urgent matter," he told the guards at the entry to the great hall.

They both nodded, and one whistled, summoning another clansman from a passing patrol. That warrior took up the guard's position so the other could escort them inside.

Not for the first time did Cailean marvel at how efficiently the McDonnels worked together to defend their stronghold and their clan. Over the centuries the laird's garrison of warriors had trained for every possibility of attack, even in the guise of two druids arriving after dark.

The guard bid them to wait with him by

the hearth in the great hall while another man was sent to the laird's tower. A smiling maid appeared with mugs of steaming brew to warm them, and after offering them a meal, returned to the kitchens.

"Fair evening Master Flen, Ovate Lusk." The massive, towering form of Tharaen Aber, the clan's seneschal, came from the tower archway. The largest man among the McDonnels, the Pritani warrior's calm nature corresponded with his unique strength-in-battle gift, which made him virtually invincible. "The laird has retired for the night. Might I help?"

Bhaltair shook his head. "Rouse him, Seneschal. This cannae hold until morning."

Raen nodded, and then smiled past the old druid. "Diana, would you keep our friends company for a moment?"

His wife, a very tall, well-built redhead dressed in a slim gown that matched her fine eyes, nodded and grinned as she came to hug the old druid. "It's way past your bedtime, Grandpa."

"Aye, but trouble never respects that," Bhaltair told her.

Cailean envied the close relationship his

master had attained with Raen's wife, a former police detective who had crossed over some two years past. While she had come from the future, Diana shared Bhaltair's bloodline. It made him yearn once more to see his own son, Danyel Gordon, who resided with his countess mother at her clan's stronghold. Since Bethany Gordon was married to the Gordons' laird, his visits to see the child had to be infrequent and discrete.

Diana chatted with his master about her latest endeavors, but Cailean hardly heard them. In his thoughts he kept seeing the huge, bare-chested man chasing the druidess through the barrier. If he were indeed Gavin McShane, and had not drowned, why would he conceal himself? How had a male from the future even managed to get to the islands? The secrecy had to be connected to his presence on Everbay, and his pursuit of the druidess. Was Quintus Seneca, tribune of the Ninth Legion, behind all of it? If the undead had somehow enthralled the pair, and used them to seek revenge against the clan, it could spell the end for the immortal McDonnels —or worse.

Diana's husband returned at last to escort them to the laird's tower. Cailean knew his master would do most of the talking, and for once he was glad. His fears preyed on him so now that he might reveal more than was wise.

Inside the laird's chamber Lachlan McDonnel stood by the mantle of his huge hearth. Beside him his wife, Kinley, sat swaddled in a dove-colored wrap. Her unbound white-gold hair and bare feet, as well as the laird's unlaced tunic, made it plain they had been abed. Still they warmly welcomed him and Bhaltair as if they were guests invited to attend them.

"Forgive us for intruding, my lord," Bhaltair said immediately, and glanced back at Raen. "If we may beg a private word."

Lachlan nodded to his seneschal, who departed. "You make a habit of this, Master Flen, so 'tis no shock. Mayhap you should consider living at Dun Aran, to avoid the frequent trips."

Bhaltair chuckled instead of taking offense, proof of how he had mellowed over the last years. "'Twould seem a solution,

Laird. But we couldnae wait with this news, of which I am unhappiest to deliver."

Once he'd related what they had discovered Kinley grinned. "But that's wonderful, Master Flen. Jema will be over the moon to find out her brother is alive."

The old druid held up one hand. "We cannae say for certain the man is Gavin McShane. Then, too, we dinnae ken the reason why he would be chasing after a druidess on an island where the undead slaughtered an entire tribe of our kind."

"The Moon Wake?" Lachlan said, and when Bhaltair nodded he glanced at his wife. "'Tis no' good news, Kinley. He may yet be under enthrallment." He regarded the old druid. "You dinnae wish Jema and Tormod to know he yet lives, or you would have summoned them. What more is there to this tale?"

As always, the laird cut to the heart of the matter, and Cailean felt his master eye him. With halting words, the young druid explained what had—and hadn't—been done with the tribe's village.

"I mean to travel to Everbay directly,"

Cailean said, "to discover who these intruders are, and what they do there. 'Twould be unwise to go without you, Master," he said to Bhaltair. "I think too we should ask Daimh Haral to join us, as he is the last of the Moon Wake tribe, and this is his natal land." He regarded the laird, whose expression had gone remote. "If you will allow some clansmen to escort us, that would provide some defense against the male, if 'tis needed."

"I'll go," Kinley said, rising from her chair. When Lachlan scowled at her she gave him a sweet smile. "I'm the only trained search and rescue professional in the clan. If this guy is Gavin, he'll respond better to someone from his own time. Stop looking like you want to tie me to the bed again. You know I'm right. Also, remember." She lifted one slim hand out of her wrap, and blue-white flames flared up from her fingertips as she demonstrated her gift of throwing fire. "I'm your best weapon of mass undead destruction."

"That doesnae mean I have to like it," the laird said, his voice gruff. "Very well, Ovate. My lady and I shall accompany you to Everbay. We were planning a trip to the mainland to meet with my allies at week's end. Once there we shall make briefer our visit, and then travel to your settlement to make the jaunt to Everbay." Lachlan put an arm around his wife's shoulders. "And pray to the gods we dinnae have to do more than bring back Gavin McShane."

Chapter Eight

THE DAY HAD passed so painfully slow that Catriona thought she might burst. Though she had gardened, mended, and cleaned house, it seemed the sun would never near the horizon. Now Catriona paced back and forth, absently stepping over Jester as he scurried alongside her. She'd finished drying her hair by the fire, and dressed in the best of her handmade gowns. The pale linen bodice and nut-hull stained wool skirts looked tidy and clean, and when she braided and put up her locks she would be at her best. That she longed for the finer, better-made garments she'd left in her wardrobe at Ennis and Senga's cottage bedeviled her. She could not ever wear such things on the island, and certainly not in front of the highlander, but she wanted to look pretty for him.

Aye, and she wanted him to kiss her again. Would he? Or had she somehow disappointed in that the first time?

As she paused Jester hopped on her shoe and chirped at her.

"You're no' helping," she told the baby puffin as she plucked him from her clog and held him up to her face. The soft brush of his down against her cheek soothed her enough to smile. "Now for your meal, and then to mine at Gavin's."

As she fed the nestling Catriona wondered what Gavin would be making for their dinner. She knew highlanders favored dishes different from islander fare, and included meat from the livestock and game. He'd done well enough with the fish he brought or caught, and she'd told him she would not eat anything feathered or furred. The best she could hope for might be a vegetable pottage and some bread, if he knew how to steam it. She should show him how to manage it in a hearth pot hung over the night's embers.

If she kept thinking about food, she'd not keep remembering that kiss on the shore, and how Gavin had pressed her against him, and the delicious, demanding way his mouth had felt on hers. Every bone in her body had been trembling when he'd lifted his head, and looked at her with those moonstone eyes, dark and filled with so much hunger. It made her thighs tighten just to recall it, and then he'd left her at the barrier, as if it had never happened.

Jester trilled, drawing her attention to where he'd settled down under her hand for a nap. She gently placed the cage basket over him before washing her hands and attending to her hair.

As she braided the long strands, she saw the eiders waddle in, their beaks clamped over some stalks of tiny, golden-hearted blooms. Since the primroses weren't something the ducks ate, she caught their thoughts up in hers.

The male showed her a blurry memory of Isela tucking blooms into her braids—something he could not possibly know. Then she understood: the eider had seen her mother in Catriona's memory.

"My thanks," she told the ducks as they dropped the blooms on the ground by her feet. They waddled back out of the cottage, satisfied that they had helped.

She had no mirror, so she had to place the flowers while looking at her dim reflection in a bowl of water. The vivid, phlox-violet of the petals made the red in her hair seem brighter, which pleased her. Gavin had favored her hair, judging by the way he'd run his fingers through it.

Would she never cease lusting after his touch, his kisses, his attention, his approval?

The slant of the sunbeams through the front window forced her to stop dithering and wrap herself in her shawl. After she banked the hearth, she gathered her courage, and marched out of the cottage.

The brown hares peeped out of their hedge to inspect her before returning to cuddle with their leverets.

"You make a lass wish to preen," she muttered as she began to walk for the barrier.

She stayed within the spell wall until she reached the entry to the forest, where she stepped through. The scent of baking bread and roasting vegetables teased her nose, and relieved a little of her apprehension. They also made her intensely curious as to what he was cooking.

She followed the trail through the trees to the clearing, where she expected to see the highlander at work over his campfire. Instead a plume of thin white smoke rose from his stone chimney. It seemed he had finished and was making use of his hearth.

Catriona smiled as she went to the open doorway and looked inside. Gavin had yet to furnish, but a large cloth had been spread over the hard-packed dirt floor. On the cloth he had arranged two plates, two goblets and a flat, round stone in the center. Two more cloths had been folded and arranged like seats. The man himself stood by the hearth, where he peered into a long slot beneath the mantle.

Catriona politely cleared her throat. As he turned around she tried not to stare at the odd mitts on his hands. "You said to come at sunset," she reminded him.

"So I did. Welcome." He removed the

mitts and came to her, bending down to kiss her cheek. "Are you hungry?"

She'd been too nervous to eat anything since rising, and the appetizing smells were making her belly feel almost painfully hollow. "A little. What do you make there?"

He started to say something, shook his head, and grinned. "I've no name for it that you would ken. 'Tis like a savory tart, with wild carrots, herbs, roasted garlic and cheese melted atop it all. There are fresh greens with fruit and berries to go with it, but let me get the tart out."

Gavin went back to the hearth, and using his mitts removed another flat, round stone with a large, golden-brown tart atop it. He brought it to the stone in the center of the cloth and let it slide from one stone to the other. He beckoned for her to sit, and retrieved a stone jug and two bowls with the greens and fruit.

Catriona inspected the tart, which had a pale, herb-flecked mash beneath the lacings of melted cheese and roasted garlic cloves. Gavin produced a blade and cut a generous wedge from it to put on her plate, and then filled her goblet with a light-colored cider from the jug.

"One of my crewmates presses sand pears and ferments the juice, but I favor it fresh." He lifted his goblet. "To good neighbors."

She joined her drink to his for the toast and then sampled the juice, which was sweet and cold. "This tart, 'tis a highland specialty?"

"'Tis a little like something I loved at home," Gavin said. "I cannae acquire all of the ingredients here, so I made do with what I had."

Before she tried the greens she surreptitiously inspected them to assure he had picked nothing poisonous or bitter, and was happy to see dandelion leaves, sorrel, sweet red clover and watercress. The blaeberries, junipers and wild cherries provided a sweet balance to the earthy greens.

"You know gathering," she told him.

"No' enough. Some mushrooms tempted me, but I didnae recognize them," Gavin said. "I thought I might try no' to poison you this first meal."

"I shall show you which are safe for eating," she promised.

He seemed anxious for her to try the tart, so she picked up the wedge and took a small bite. The herbed carrot mash provided a sweet note to the piquant cheese and the richness of the browned garlic, the latter of which melted like spicy butter on her tongue.

"Give up fishing," Catriona finally said. "I shall hire you to cook for me every night."

He laughed, and the sound moved through her like currents of deep, satisfying joy.

As they ate Gavin told her about the work he had done to complete the roof thatching, and his next task of fashioning the furniture he would need. He favored pine, which saved her from warning him against culling any of the oak trees on the far side of the island.

"Pine boughs work well for a bed frame, although with your size you may want them thick and sturdy," Catriona told him. "For the ticking you'll need rope to weave the bottom, but treat it first with pine sap, so the cords last longer."

"I'll need more hand tools before I start on the furniture, and I'm no' sure if I want to put in floor planks or settle for rushes. I have such plans, but no' knowing if they'll do. Any advice you would offer is welcome." He drained his goblet and glanced at her empty plate. "Have you left room for a sweet?"

"Aye, but I change my mind. You cannae cook for me," she told him gravely. "For I shall eat myself into a whale."

"That would take more than I've to offer." He eyed her narrow waist before he rose and brought a bowl of roasted nuts gleaming with a golden coating. "I cannae promise you these will be as tasty as the rest. They were a gamble."

Catriona gingerly picked up one of the sticky nuts, and took a bite. He had roasted them and rolled them in honey. She closed her eyes for a moment, licking the golden drops from her fingertips, before she regarded him.

"Then again I might like being a whale."

Gavin grinned, and leaned forward to brush his mouth against hers. Though his kiss had been unexpected, her lips clung to his as she shared the taste of the honey. But all too soon he drew back.

"I've one more day before I must go to

Hrossey," he said. "Will you go gathering with me in the morning?"

Catriona thought of the portrait he'd drawn and burned. Is she still in his heart? Was she the reason he treated a kiss like a blow? "Aye, if you wish."

She helped him tidy up after their meal, and let him walk her back to the edge of the glen. He'd brought an extra torch, which he lit from his own before handing it to her.

"So you dinnae fall in the spring." He plucked one of the primroses from her hair, and drew its soft petals across her lips. "I came here to be alone, Catriona. To heal the wounds from the wretched mistakes I've made. Now here you are, as lovely and sweet a lass as a man could want. You make me wish for more, but I cannae." He touched her cheek. "No' yet."

He was going to break her heart without even trying, Catriona thought. She covered his hand with hers briefly, then took it in a firm clasp.

"Then we shall be friends," she told him briskly. "I will show you the island when I am come here, and you will look out for my friends when I'm away." She wrinkled her nose at him. "Tomorrow morn, we hunt mushrooms and angelica and scurvy leaf, and I shall show you a place you cannae find on your own."

His brows arched. "Scurvy leaf?"

"'Tis spicy and hot, like white radish, and very good stuffing for any fish. Sailors chew the leaves to keep from falling sick on long voyages." She prodded his shoulder. "And you a fisherman."

"My thanks, lass," he said, sounding almost depressed.

"Fair night, neighbor."

She kept up her smile as she stepped through the barrier, and then blinked until the sting in her eyes abated. Of course she wanted a man who couldnae feel the same for her. Of course. She was as much a ghost as her kin.

Chapter Nine

ALTHOUGH SHE HAD planned to return home, Catriona sent a messenger bird through the portal to Ennis and Senga that she would be remaining on the island. She felt a twinge of guilt when she added no explanation as to why, but she often extended her stays, so the delay would not trouble them. Hiding Gavin's presence on the island seemed wiser than giving her family a new reason to worry.

It also gave Catriona a sense of having him all to herself, like a wonderful secret.

The day after the meal he'd cooked for her it rained from sunrise to dusk, but she took some cording to Gavin's cottage to show him how to knot a base for the bed he would build.

He in turn made a pottage with fish, brown crab and scallops, flavored with garlic and sorrel, to go with the herbed bannocks and smoked silver darlings she'd brought for him.

"No, I'll surely burst," she told him when he tried to refill her bowl.

"Seeing you eat well makes me feel less a glutton." Reluctantly he added the last from the pot to his bowl. "Tell me, when do you leave for home?"

"As it happens I sent word to my family that I'd be staying a wee bit longer." Feeling a little shy now, she nibbled on the last piece of her bannock until she thought of his work. "You'll be for Hrossey on the morrow."

"Aye. We're for a far run this trip, so I'll no' return for two or threeday." He eyed her. "I ken 'tis your island, Cat, but I cannae like leaving you alone here."

Catriona chuckled. "I've been so twenty years, Gavin. I'll come to no harm. 'Tis more likely you will when *I* go back."

Her joke made him fall silent as he finished his pottage, but Catriona felt a tingle of pleasure. Gavin didn't care for the prospect of her leaving the island. That was not the sentiment of a man who wished to be left alone.

But the next day, as he'd said, Gavin left on the dawn ferry for Hrossey. The prospect of threeday waiting for him did not please her, but neither did visiting Ennis and Senga so short a time. As she'd done before she busied herself, but this time with the garden. Nothing helped to lift a gloomy spirit more than spending time among the blooms and digging her fingers into the rich soil. Even so, she couldn't help but look to the horizon. And to her delight, he returned that evening before dusk. When she saw him walking from the dock, she scooped up the angelica she had cut by the spring. She all but skipped down the path to meet him.

"Were there no fish to catch today?" she teased.

"No boat from which to fish. The Mollers sailed to Shetland to settle a family dispute. I've no work but here until midweek next." He shouldered his pack and nodded at her gathering basket. "Is that hogweed?"

She shook her head. "Angelica. They look much alike, but you'll no' want to be eating the other. I'm making jam of these for my oatcakes. There's still light enough to go foraging, if you'd want."

"I'd want." His moonstone eyes shifted over her. "Will you meet me at the forest trail?"

Catriona agreed, and they parted ways. Once she returned to her village and put the angelica to soak in cool water, she changed into her oldest gown, and retrieved her hand wraps and foraging sacks. She felt all aflutter with excitement that Gavin had returned early, and would not have to leave again for four or fiveday.

She would not push herself on him, of course. He wanted his healing time, and she had to respect that. She hoped by showing him the island's many treasures it would help him forget the sorrows that had driven him here. Everbay had always done so for her.

Once he was happy again, then perhaps they might become more than friendly neighbors.

Catriona hurried along the barrier toward the forest, where she saw Gavin already standing in wait for her. He'd changed into older garments as well, and the soft old linen tunic clung to his broad shoulders like a second skin. The sun poured over him like liquid amber, making him seem almost god-like. For a moment she stood behind the barrier so she could admire him without his notice, and felt her body warm and soften as she did.

Gods, but he drew her like a bee to a bloom. Would he ever see her as the woman she was?

"I can feel you there," he said, startling her. "Is something amiss?"

Her head, Catriona thought as she stepped through the spell wall. "I was thinking on where I might take you. To forage," she added quickly as she handed him a sack and some of the wraps.

"I'd like mushrooms to stuff my next fish," he said, watching her wind the strips of hemp weave around her palms. He did the same, but had difficulty folding in the ends.

"Dinnae scowl, for you'll want these when we find nettle." Catriona secured the wraps for him. "Even the young ones sting."

He grunted. "Then why gather them?"

"Soaking them removes the bane. With their flowers they make a fine morning brew." She stepped back to inspect him. "The fibers can too be retted and woven into cloth, if you've a loom."

"A weaver I'm no'," he admitted.

She laughed. "'Tis less work to make the tea."

From there she led him along the older, partially-overgrown path to the sunnier side of his forest, where the rowans and willows hemmed each side of the burbling stream. There she showed him how to search fallen limbs and logs for the morels, goldies and other fungi that were safe to eat.

"Where you find pink millers, you should also see ceps," she told him, pointing to the two different growths. "Ceps like to hide, but they peep a bit of white underside, so you must kneel to spot them."

He learned quickly, and noticed that goldies favored growing on birch trunks while ceps preferred to sprout in the rotting leaf beds carpeting the trees' roots. He knew enough not to pick every mushroom, leaving plenty behind to shed their spores. He was also quick to spot which poisonous growths closely resembled those safe to eat.

"If you cannae tell, dinnae take it," Catriona said once they had collected enough to eat and dry without waste. "Or bring it to me. I ken everything that grows here." The shift in his expression made her frown. "I dinnae boast, Gavin. I've roamed the forests and slopes and shores all of my life."

"But to come here, alone, as just a wee lass." He shook his head. "You might have fallen from a cliff, or drowned in the spring."

Catriona smiled a little as she recalled some of the scrapes she'd gotten herself into, those first years. "Each time I visited, the island taught me a new way to look after myself. 'Twas no' always pleasant, but those lessons made me stronger, and smarter."

"Your family shouldnae have allowed it," Gavin said, his tone stern. "'Tis unforgiveable."

Unforgiveable? If only he knew.

Run to the falls, Catriona. Dinnae let your uncle see you. Hurry, lass.

He saw her reaction and frowned. "I spoke

without thought. My people protect the young from harm."

The memory of her mother's final words made bile rise in her throat. "So did my family." She pushed back the sick feeling and regarded him. "Come, and I'll show you where you will find more goldies than you may eat in a year."

Chapter Ten

AS HE ROSE from his silk-strewn bed Daimh Haral felt again the weight of his years. Old age pains had begun attacking the joints of his knees and shoulders, which had grown so stiff now he often had to partake of more poppy juice than was wise. As he glanced down at the white satin of his pillow, he saw a cluster of thin, silver and red hairs that had fallen out of his scalp. At this rate he would be bald within the year. With an angry jerk he covered the self-indulgence of his bed linens with a plain, woven coverlet and hobbled out into his front room.

A hiss greeted him from the large, rope-bound basket by the hearth, which tipped side to side as its occupant stretched.

"Wanting your breakfast, Anoup?" Daimh murmured as he went into the cold pantry and retrieved one of the dead mice he stored there. He carried it to the basket, releasing the ties and removing the lid. With a grin he dangled the rodent by the tail over the opening.

Anoup reared its large head, flicking the air with its forked tongue. Daimh had paid dearly to have the viper smuggled from Francia to Scotland, but its venom had proven invaluable for certain rituals. He also considered the snake as the best of companions, as it was silent, mostly docile and needed to be fed only once every few weeks.

Dark striations on its umber scales twisted as it reached for the mouse. Daimh amused himself by shifting the small carcass just out of the viper's reach, until it hissed a warning.

"Very well, have it." He dropped the mouse on the snake's head, and chuckled as Anoup struck and injected its venom. "Good lad."

He made sure to cover and secure the basket before putting his kettle to boil on the fire and returning to his room to dress. Living among another druid tribe had been a trial, but he had successfully concealed from them his ongoing work with exotic magics. Summoning dark forces had to be done away from the settlement, of course, but he had long ago created protected niches where he could cast as he pleased. The many attempts he had made to discover the reason for his single enormous failing, however, had yet to bear results. He could not permit his body to die before he found the answer, either.

Under no circumstances could Daimh disincarnate and return to the well of stars. He would spend eternity in the kind of torment that made what he himself had done to his blood kin look like a thoughtful kindness.

Daimh changed out of his nightshirt, despairing as he looked down at the densely-inked cyphers now fading on his age-spotted flesh and withering muscle. He had devoted himself to the study of ancient magics, and collected scrolls written by the *remetch en Kermet*, the People of the Black Land. From them he had distilled the designs of his skinwork, which he'd inked on himself in secret. The hundreds of centuries their priests had devoted to their all-consuming cult of the dead had produced a wealth of powerful magics and spells. Each time he used one of their rituals he felt the brush of energy so archaic and colossal it staggered him. To be the master of such power would enable him to rule over druid kind for all eternity.

First he had to defeat Death itself.

He slowly pulled on a clean robe, and took from his belt a vial of poppy juice to mix into his morning brew. His hand quivered until he clutched it tightly around the slender stone ampoule. Then came a jag of power from his house wards as they reacted to the presence of two approaching druids. Quickly he uncorked the vial, swallowed the bitter contents and then smoothed down his thinning hair. The smile he forced onto his mouth he had practiced for years. It aped a natural good humor that completely deceived his fellow druids. They would pick up nothing more from him, thanks to the arcane symbols inked on his body.

Daimh quickly dispelled the house wards,

opened his door, and hailed the two druids. "Fair morning, Master Flen. Ovate Lusk, you're near full-grown now. Come in, come in."

He hustled the grave-faced men into his cottage, chattering as he did about the fine spring they were having and the promise of bountiful crops for the settlement. As expected his false cheer deepened the other men's gloom, from which he took some silent satisfaction.

"Sit, sit." He fussed over them, bringing them mugs of brew as he nattered on about coming rituals and gatherings for which he cared nothing. "But enough of my gossip," he said when the ovate began to fidget. "What brings you to me this fine day?"

The old druid's expression was that of a man kicked in the belly. "Daimh, we wouldnae disturb you with this, but as the last of the Harals, 'tis only right that you hear what we have learned."

He swallowed a sour laugh. He *was* the reason he was the last of the Harals. Slowly, he let his smile fade. "'Tis a daily struggle to go on, but I do my best, to honor my blood kin. What have you to tell me?"

The younger druid told him of the breach of the protective barrier on Everbay, and the two intruders discovered as the cause. One, thought to be the twin brother of a member of the McDonnel clan, had been pursuing a young female through the boundary.

"The lass is unknown to us," Cailean added once he finished the tale. "But she has the look of your tribe."

"May the gods have answered my entreaties." A Haral, yet alive. The dark gods had indeed shown him favor. Daimh tucked his hands in his sleeves before he clenched them to stop their shaking. "Describe her to me, please, Brother."

"She is tall, slender, and long-limbed," the younger man said. "Her hair is a fiery brown, and her eyes blue-violet in color. She runs like a deer."

Now it came clear to him why the Anubis ritual had never bestowed on him physical immortality. He had made a terrible mistake with the sacrifice, but that could be corrected.

"Could she be your kin?" Cailean asked, dragging him from his brooding thoughts.

Now he would have to choose his words carefully, for both druids would sense a lie. "I cannae tell you, but I would be very glad to meet the lass in person."

"We shall travel to the island with Laird McDonnel and his lady wife at week's end," Bhaltair said gently. "As you ken the island better than any, we would ask you to join us."

Daimh let tears of relief fill his eyes. "Oh, Brother. If only you ken what this means to me." He drew a kerchief from his pocket and dabbed at his eyes. "Forgive me, Brothers. I am growing old, and to return to the place where every one of my family were butchered…'twill require much preparation of the spirit."

The two druids exchanged a look before Bhaltair nodded. "Only ken that we must keep this journey a secret from all others. 'Tis much unknown about what we will find there."

He didn't have to feign his happy smile this time. "Believe me, Brother, such secrets I can keep, very well."

Chapter Eleven

SHOWING GAVIN ALL the treasures of the island occupied most of Catriona's time while he was out of work, and becoming his teacher made her feel contented and happy. The highlander was not only a quick learner, but possessed the natural druid appreciation for nature and all its wonders. They worked together effortlessly, too, as if they had known each other all their lives.

Once she felt sure he would not gather anything poisonous, she took him around the island's shores to show him the best spots for fishing, collecting and swimming. They were wading through the shallows one day when a long, dark shadow appeared in the water, and Gavin grabbed her up in his arms.

"There's a shark's fin," he said, and turned to carry her back to the shore.

"Aye, but it willnae attack us. Put me down." When he did she pointed to the creature's triangular snout and gaping, white-striated mouth. "He has teeth, but he doesnae use them for feeding. See how he gulps water as he swims? 'Tis a basker."

Catriona sent her thoughts to the big fish, making it clear that they meant no harm to it, and the massive creature swam deep, surfacing and propelling itself completely above the water before crashing down and splashing them with a huge wave.

Gavin laughed as he wiped the sodden hair back from her face and then his. "Was that the fish's way of saying 'Fair day' or something less polite?"

She wrinkled her nose. "We're muddying his water, I think."

That had been a fine day, and only when they parted at the barrier did Catriona feel a little melancholy. It became harder each time they separated not to seek some excuse to offer Gavin a kiss or an embrace, but she was determined to remain simply the friendly neighbor he wanted.

She also felt sure they would not be only that for much longer. Often when he thought she didn't notice he looked at her face and body with admiring eyes. He also constantly found reasons to take her hand or elbow, and sometimes even wrapped an arm around her shoulders. Every touch became a little torment, and when she finally sought her bed at night she would remember how it felt to have his hands on her.

The unpredictable island weather often cut short their walks, but Gavin always invited her back to the cottage to have a hot brew or simple meal and talk. He made her laugh with his stories about his crewmates, and sigh when he described watching the sun rise over the sea from the deck of the fisher. He found peace in his work, she could tell that, but he seemed to still be yearning for something more.

Catriona hoped, more than anything, that he felt the same need she did.

She helped him find good, sturdy pines to use for his furnishings, and taught him to collect the resins and needles to use as cord coating and basket-making. His big hands were strong and dexterous, but he proved to be a poor basket-maker.

"You'd do better to carve them from wood," Catriona advised him when his latest attempt fell apart in her hands. She nodded at the fine bed frame he had just finished pegging together. "That will last a hundred years."

"I'll need more birch bark to pad the underside of the ticking, or that will last no more than a month," he told her. "I saw some bigger trees at the south end of the stream. Have you ever harvested from them?"

A jab of pain made her heart ache. "I've no', but there are plenty near the falls."

"You've a waterfall on the island?" His eyes lit up when she nodded. "Will you show me the way there?"

Catriona knew if she refused he would want to know why, so she forced a smile. "If you wish, of course."

Gavin wanted to go the very next day, and

when she took him down the old path she noticed everything that haunted her dreams.

"This is the prettiest path," he said to her. "I've no' seen so many berry bushes on the other side." He glanced at her. "Are you well, little Cat? You look pale."

"I didnae sleep much last night." Leading him to the spill of the stream down a rocky slope gave Catriona time to calm herself, at least until she saw the white torrents of the falls.

"Gods above," Gavin said, leaning over to look down at the churning pool below. "'Tis incredible."

The scent and sound of the water sent tremors through her middle, but Catriona ignored them. "The goldies love damp, so they are bountiful around the falls. See them?" She pointed to the thick mushroom clusters on either side of the water. "If you dry the pale green moss from the rocks, and stuff it in your boots, 'twill take away smells and damp." And if she never had to come here again, it would be the delight of her life.

"Your voice is shaking," Gavin said and turned her to face him. "Cat?"

A sudden clap of thunder made her jerk away from him and shake her head. "I'm only weary."

He frowned up at the darkening skies. "We'll no' make it back to the cottage before the rain comes." He looked around them. "Do you ken a spot we can shelter until the storm passes?"

The air darkened, and suddenly Catriona was a little lass again, running with stubbed toes and twigs snarled in her hair. That night the cries and the snarls of dying and killing had chased after her through the trees, and every shadow had seemed enormous and filled with hands. Somehow, she'd found her way to the very edge of the falls, where Isela had shown her what they concealed.

This shall be your secret haven, Catriona. I've left all you should need inside. If trouble comes, you must run here and hide until it is daylight. Then do as I have shown you.

Her mother's mouth had gone thin, the way it did whenever Tavish argued with his brother. *Aye, Mama. But will you come for me?*

If I can, I shall.

A bright jagged light sliced down from the

sky, striking a birch near them as the air boomed with thunder and exploding bark. Without thinking Catriona grabbed Gavin by the hand and dragged him into the falls.

Blinded briefly by the pounding cascade, Catriona felt Gavin stumble and propped her shoulder under his arm to support him. Once they were inside the cave, she guided him away from the splash of the falls to the largest of the flat rocks.

"Here." She put her arm around his waist and sat with him, staying close as she peered at the scant light filtering through the falls. "They willnae find us here. 'Tis safe."

His big arm came around her, and suddenly she was sobbing into his chest. "'Twill be well now, my sweet Cat. No one is on the island but us."

She let her tears add to the sodden condition of his tunic, but only for a few moments. "I am crazed," she told him as she swiped at her face and drew back. "'Twas an unhappy memory."

"Poor lass." Gavin stroked her arm. "Who were they, that frightened you so?"

Catriona almost told him before another lightning strike illuminated the cave, revealing the little drawings she'd made on the far wall. The words caught in her tight throat as she stared at the stick people scratched into the stone, one for every member of the lost tribe. The marks had been her only comfort while she'd hidden here, and even then, she'd been too afraid to talk to them. Making even one sound might lure Uncle to her. Beneath the crude drawings was the small pallet she'd slept on, along with the old linens and blankets she'd hid under every night.

Now here she sat, about to pour her heart out to this man, and reveal to him secrets and sorrows she had protected all her life. In return he'd told her that he wished to be alone, to heal from wounds left by another woman. She did not even know from where he had come in the highlands. Her uncle had friends there, among some of the other druid tribes. Loneliness had made her more than foolish. It had lured her to the brink of disaster.

"Did my uncle send you?" She bolted to

her feet and backed away from him. "Tell me."

Gavin shook his head, his brow furrowed as he rose from the stone. "I came here by my choice. I dinnae ken who you mean, Catriona. I willnae harm you. Come to me."

"No." When he reached for her she moved back. "You've no room in your heart for me. I'm naught to you. You've no right to me."

She spun on her heel and plunged through the cascade, her boots sliding on the slippery rocks as she ran from the cave. Outside the rain poured over her as if the world had become one great fall, pounding and cold. She dodged limbs and brush as she fought her way through the forest, stumbling and falling as the rain lashed her.

Strong hands snatched her up from the ground, and Gavin lifted her off her feet, carrying her under a dense tree as she struggled. There he put her down but held her until she slumped against him.

"What did your uncle do to you?" Gavin demanded, putting her at arm's length. "Why are you so afraid of him? Catriona, tell me."

"He wants me dead, for what I saw him

do," she said, staring into his blazing eyes. "There, now you ken. Leave me and go back to your cottage now. Be alone, Gavin, and draw your woman, and burn her image again. 'Tis what you want, to drown yourself in sorrow."

As she tried to walk away he snatched her back in his arms.

"What I *want?*" he echoed, looking all over her drenched hair and dripping face. "I want peace, but I have none of it here. I listen and watch for you every moment. You dance through my days and torment my nights. I dream of you, naked and welcoming, on me, under me, everywhere. When you are with me I cannae come close, for fear I shall do this." He pressed her against his big, hard body.

Catriona wanted to slap him, but he felt so good she could only cling. "You said naught to me. Never once."

"'Twas my stupit attempt to protect you. I told myself you're no' for me. That I'm too scarred and angry for such a precious thing. That my heart hasnae room for you, for anyone." He cradled her chin. "Yet every time I touch you, you make me forget all but this."

He stroked his thumb over the trembling curves of her lips.

"I must go." Catriona slid her hands up to his shoulders to brace herself, and stood on her toes to kiss him farewell.

That brush of her mouth brought his hand to the back of her head, and he held her as he kissed her in return. The sweetness flared into passion, exploding between them like the lightning strikes. Gavin took her mouth with so much hunger she moaned, as tormented as she was thrilled. He braced himself against the tree as he lifted her higher, molding her against the unyielding toughness of his body so she could not escape him.

Catriona didn't try. She didn't want the feeling to end.

She felt so much she couldn't think. She could only cling to him as his hands shifted to her bottom and he buried his mouth against her throat. He moved her so that her throbbing mound rubbed against the stiff ridge of his erection, making her pearl swell and her sheath go slick.

He heaved in a breath and raised his head. "I've tried, lass. Tried and failed. I cannae keep from you. If you dinnae want this, tell me now."

His voice had dropped to a deep, rough growl, and something snarling and starved glittered in his moonstone eyes. Catriona should have cowered, but his beast called to her own wildness. She had conquered some part of him, a silent battle she hadn't even known she was fighting. Of course, she had to go, but she would not leave Everbay like this. The aching and longing for him would never end.

And she'd never find the strength to stay away.

"I want you, Gavin." She reached down with one hand to hike up her skirts, baring her drawers and the open seam over her sex. With streams of cold rain pouring around them she should have felt wet and miserable, but her whole body had caught fire. "Come into me, please."

Gavin lifted her again, reaching between their bodies to shove down his trews. Catriona clutched his tunic as she looked down, seeing the swollen bulb of his cockhead as he freed it and pressed it into her folds. The invasion felt rough and hot and deliciously hard, and she melted over him, her breasts jutting against his chest as he penetrated her.

Gods, but he was so wide that if she had not been so ready he might have hurt. Instead he filled her, thrusting up with his hips as she came down on his shaft. She could feel him shaking now, his muscles knotting as he tried to control his need. Tucking her leg around his waist, she worked herself down on him, stretching herself over his heavy girth. At last she felt the root of him press against her outer folds, and dropped her brow against his shoulder. Her body gripped him, caressing him from within as she tightened to feel every inch of him.

A groan rumbled up from the vault of his chest. "Catriona, dinnae. Ah, fack."

The heartfelt curse made her swell with feminine delight, and she put her lips by his ear. "Take me, Gavin, as you've wanted. As you've dreamed."

His strong arms gripped her by the waist, and shook as he lifted her up and thrust her down on him. The iron of his shaft stoked the heat of her quim, and sent shocks of bright sensation up through her belly and into her breasts. The unfettered mounds begin to bounce with every plunge he took into her, and Catriona rolled her shoulders back. She wanted him to see her breasts and their tight, red nipples through the thin, sodden stuff of her bodice.

Gavin turned, splaying his hands over her back as he pressed her against the tree. His weight shifted as he plowed deeply into her, and Catriona cried out as she saw his eyes fill with ghostly fire.

"Aye, my sweet Cat," he said, uttering a rasping growl as he worked his shaft in and out of her with heavy, almost brutal strokes. "I've all you want and more. Take my cock, take it in that tight quim, that's the way my lass."

Gavin attacked her throat, first licking and then grazing his teeth over her skin. He took hold of her flesh where her neck and shoulder joined, and sucked. She jerked at the front of her wet bodice, frantic to bear herself to his maddening mouth as he facked her faster and harder. He fastened his teeth on the thin linen and ripped it apart before he enveloped one aching nipple with his mouth.

Seeing and feeling the hot, wet ravishing power of his lips on her breast pushed Catriona past flailing need into swelling torment. The pumping, pummeling length of his cock between her thighs and the hungry ravishment of his mouth were going to drive her mad. She grabbed the long hair at the back of his head, pushing his head against her mound just as he raked his teeth over her nipple.

Gavin buried himself in her, pressing her down on him as her body filled with arcs of sweet, hot bliss. The power of the explosion of pleasure made the world go gray and dim around them. Now they were the lightning, and as she shook through the jolts of white-hot fiery delight she squeezed his shaft, and felt it swell even larger before it began to jet deep inside her softness.

"There now, there I am, there you are." His voice had gone so rough he barely formed the words. His breath washed over her throat and cheek as he jerked her from the tree and dropped with her.

Catriona straddled his lap, heaving in every breath as she rode the last, long waves of sensation. Gavin gathered her against him, his heat wrapping around her with his arms, and held her as he leaned back against the tree.

She pillowed her cheek with his shoulder, and watched as the rain finally abated to a dense mist. Beyond them the falls still roared, but all the unhappy memories the place invoked had thinned and faded. From this day she would think of it as the place where she'd made love with her highlander.

"You're so lovely," he murmured, and rubbed his palm slowly along her back. "You make me wish we'd met before…"

Her, Catriona finished for him silently. A reminder that the man's heart belonged to another.

And now she had to leave him and the island, before anything more happened, and Daimh learned that she yet lived.

Slowly she rose, hating herself as she stood and shook down her skirts. She tucked her torn bodice back over her breasts and smiled down at him. "I must attend to myself."

He frowned. "I'll go with you."

"'Twill no' take long. 'Tis naught but a short walk." She hoped he would think she meant to go and tidy herself, and it seemed he did, for he gave her a drowsy smile.

"I'll be waiting," Gavin said and caught her hand and pressed his mouth to the back of it. "Dinnae be long, sweet Cat."

She touched his cheek, nodded her lie, and left him there.

The trail to the falls forked away from them, and she followed the old path as if she meant to go down to the pool. Then she walked from it through the forest to what appeared to be a sheer cliff. She sidled into an opening at the base, and through the underground passage it guarded. Her tribe had spent years tunneling through the stone. At the other end she emerged into an ancient grove, where massive, twisted oaks grew in a circle around what her mother had called journey stones.

They shall take you wherever you wish to go, Daughter. You have only to think of the place. If I dinnae come for you, you must use the stones and leave Everbay.

As she stepped into the grove, Catriona

glanced over her shoulder. Gavin would come looking for her, but he would not be able to find the cliff entrance. The only other person alive who knew of it was her uncle.

The first time she had stumbled into the grove she had been starved and cold and terrified. She'd heard Uncle's voice in every sound, saw his shape in every shadow. She dimly remembered throwing herself into the circle of stones, but she hadn't thought of any place to go. She hadn't known any other place but home. The gods had swept her through the portal, a threshing tunnel of circling oaks, and then she landed in a ditch filled with snow. There she lay, sobbing into her numb hands until Ennis had come upon her.

What do you here, little lass?

She'd run from him into the fields, where she'd crawled into a hayrick and huddled until he'd come with the sweet cakes, and Senga. They'd tempted her out into the open, just as the highlander had.

But she was a woman now, not a wee, helpless lass.

Catriona could smell Gavin on her, like some dark potion. She wanted to run back to him, and tuck herself in his arms, and sleep with him under the stars. She could see herself with him in his cottage, like a wife, cooking and caring for him. She'd happily share his bed, and swell with his bairns, and help him forget the woman who'd broken his heart. They could have a life together, just like her mother and father had. Until Gavin spoke of her and their bairns and their happy life to the wrong man, and word reached her uncle that she was still alive.

Then he would come to kill them all.

Forcing her legs to take the last steps into the stone circle demanded all of her strength. She wrapped her arms around her waist, and closed her eyes for a moment as she envisioned the grove just beyond the old cottage where she had found safety at last.

The portal opened, enveloping her in light and darkness as she fell through it.

After so many trips Catriona had learned how to arrive on her feet. A clear blue sky filled with soft, thin white clouds stretched over her head. The grass here in the highlands was thinner and shorter, but wildflowers still abounded. She walked from the clearing and through the oaks to the long, narrow green pasture where Ennis's old dun mare stood placidly cropping.

"Fair day, Glenna." She patted the mare's short nose before she started across the pasture for the cottage that had been her haven since childhood.

No one looking at the old loch-stone house would think it grand. Part of the roof wanted mending, and the chimney stood slightly askew. Yet surrounding the cottage grew beds of flowers, herbs, vegetables and berry bushes in such profusion they looked as if they guarded it. That was thanks to Ennis, who had such an affinity for growing things that he could push a twig in the ground and it would sprout leaves.

A tall, thin figure walked out of the back garden, his narrow face lighting up as soon as he saw her. "Well, now. You've come back early." He pushed back a lock of his greying red hair, and then his fox-brown eyes shifted down and his happiness vanished. "What happened to you, lass?"

"I'm well, Ennis." Suddenly remembering

her torn bodice, she tucked an arm across her breasts. "I had a mishap."

"And you're soaked through." He hurried over, taking off his coat to drape around her, adding his arm across her back as he urged her toward the back door. "Come inside by the fire, before you catch a chill."

Catriona managed to keep smiling until they entered the cottage, and she saw Senga sitting in her chair by the hearth mending one of her weeding baskets. Short and stout, with her silvery fair hair woven in a crown of braids, her bow of a mouth turned up and then down.

"Bless me." The plump woman put aside her basket. "We didnae expect you for days yet, lass. No' that I mind. You've been away too long this visit." She glared at her husband. "Dinnae tell me you kept her out in the garden nattering when she's all but drenched."

"I brought her in directly," he assured her. "Didnae I, Moggy?"

"Aye." Hearing her old childhood nickname made Catriona tear up. "Forgive me, I didnae mean to...I had..." The excuses knotted in her throat, and she covered her face with her shaking hands.

Senga came over to take her in her arms, and made soothing noises as she led her toward her bed chamber. "We'll get you into something dry and warm. Ennis, go and make the lass a warming brew."

Chapter Twelve

THE THUD OF approaching hobnail boots in the outer passage distracted Quintus from the illuminated manuscript he was trying without success to decipher. He closed the ancient text and rubbed his tired eyes. He'd forgotten to feed again, but these days even his hunger for blood barely registered.

"Come in," he called a moment after a knock sounded.

His prefect entered and pulled back his hood as he knelt and saluted. In his right hand he held one of the tiny scrolls used to relay messages from the mainland.

Quintus suspected it wouldn't contain

anything of interest to him, but he still had to act his part. "What is it?"

"A message sent by an ally of your predecessor, Tribune." Strabo stood and offered the scroll.

Gaius Lucinius had made few friends outside the legion, and even fewer among his own men. Feeling a twinge of curiosity, Quintus took the scroll and unrolled it to read the small, delicate script inside. He read it twice more before he glared at Strabo.

"Has this been verified as genuine?"

"It has," the prefect said and described an older druid hand-delivering the message to the enthralled mortal keeper of their messenger birds on the mainland.

Quintus eyed the signature on the scroll. "Are you familiar with this druid Daimh Haral?"

Strabo's upper lip curled. "I know that our former tribune made a pact with the man to aid him in attacking an island settlement. For what purpose, I cannot tell you, but we carried out the raid, and killed every member of the tribe."

"Except Haral," Quintus corrected as he stroked his chin.

"Whatever the druid wants, I advise against entering into another pact," Strabo said. "He is a traitor to his own kind. He would not hesitate to betray the legion."

"Ah, but the reward he offers is one I find hard to ignore." Taking pity on the prefect, he offered him the scroll. "See for yourself."

Strabo's good eye darted back and forth as he read the message. "He offers the McDonnel laird in exchange for the son of a mortal." He met Quintus's gaze. "Why would he want the child?"

"What does it matter to us?" He smiled a little. "If Haral could deliver the laird for such a modest price, I think we might at last find the highlanders' stronghold. One night, one massive strike by the entire legion, and our enemy will finally pay for all they've done to us."

"The entire legion is at quarter-strength, Tribune." The prefect crumpled the scroll in his fist. "We barely match the McDonnel's numbers, and we are easier to kill than they are. We cannot hope to prevail. It would be the end of us."

A dull anger rose inside Quintus's chest. "You forever mewl about protecting the men. This is how we do that—forever. When we destroy the clan, we will remove the only hindrance to taking Scotland and all its mortals for our own."

"Half of the men have never engaged the McDonnels in battle," Strabo persisted. "There is only so much I can train them to do. They have no real experience."

The tribune shot to his feet and went toe-to-toe with the other man. "Are you a Roman soldier or a cringing woman?"

Strabo's scarred mouth worked for a moment before he dropped his gaze. "I am a prefect of the Ninth. I do not cower. I do not run."

Quintus deliberately put his hand on the unmarked side of Strabo's face. "When I look at you, I see the endurance. The gods know you have suffered, as do I. I made you prefect to honor what you sacrificed. I have done all I can for you, and you sneer and caper and back step every time we are presented with risk. Where is your courage, Titus? Where is the centurion who served the legion with strength and honor? Did Freyja's Eye burn it out of you along with half your face?"

Strabo's mouth peeled back from his teeth, and he went down on his knees to prostrate himself. "I am your man, Tribune. My heart and my sword are yours. Give the word, and I shall see it done."

Quintus didn't hear anything but sincerity in his voice and his posture. At the same time, he thought Strabo had said and done exactly what a high-ranking officer whose loyalty was in doubt would do to preserve his own hide.

"This is how it will be: we will take the child, and secure the capture of Lachlan McDonnel," Quintus told him. "Once we have him, we will use him to get to the rest of the clan, and eliminate them all. Then, Prefect, we will have the world to enthrall."

Strabo lifted his scarred face, and produced a convincing if grotesque smile. "As you command, Tribune."

Outside the tribune's door Bryn moved from her listening post down the passage, taking care to tread silently until she was out of earshot. The guards she and Strabo had instructed to keep watch inclined their heads as she passed them. She would have felt joyous, had she still been able to feel anything but deep, abiding loathing for Quintus Seneca.

Bryn returned to the training area, and used her mortal thralls to summon her ladies to her private chamber. The tribune had provided her with all the luxuries and comforts that a courtesan might desire, but Bryn didn't care for the rich silk gowns and costly furnishings. Her bed slave, an eager young sailor she kept naked and chained by the hearth, roused from his sleep and immediately grew erect.

"My goddess." He crawled over, his swelling penis bobbing as he tried to kiss her bare feet. "Permit me see to yer pleasure, I beg ye."

At first his perpetual adoration and desire had amused Bryn, who had been well-used but never loved. Now it simply drove home yet another reminder of what Quintus Seneca had taken from her along with her mortal life.

"I might have found a widower wanting a companion," she told her thrall as she idly wound a piece of her hair around her finger. "A rich old man with no family, who would have appreciated my skills, and left me his fortune. There were some who came through my village."

The sailor nodded eagerly. "Aye, Mistress, for ye are a beauty rare. None could resist ye."

She glanced down at him as he spread kisses all over her foot. "Dinnae make me kill you tonight."

Her ladies arrived a short time later, and she sent the thrall out to be fed. She checked that the hallway was empty, then closed and bolted the door before turning to the other women.

"Quintus Seneca and Titus Strabo are squabbling over a druid who offers the McDonnel laird to them," Bryn said. "If they strike a bargain, they'll have to leave Staffa to make the exchange."

Gerda and Jean, both of whom had been badly used as thralls, exchanged a look.

"It could be our chance," Gerda said, her dark eyes sparkling.

"We must take it," Jean agreed, as the other ladies nodded.

"Aye," Bryn said. "'Twould seem our time soon arrives, but first we must make ready. Begin selecting the newly-arrived and enthrall them. Have them bring enough food and water to keep them alive for a moon."

Gerda frowned. "Won't they be missed by the procurer, Mistress?"

"I've seen to it that Strabo will deal with him," Bryn said and looked around the room at the determined faces of her ladies. "Remember to be generous with the men. We cannae have them doubting for a moment our devotion to their pricks."

"At least I dinnae have to fack Strabo," Jean said, grimacing. "I cannae envy you that, Mistress."

"Aye, for he looks like a leper, and swives like a bull," Bryn said and smiled at her. "But his true hunger is for the tribune's heart, buried around his dagger."

"Do you think he'll kill Seneca for us, Mistress?" one of the younger whores asked.

"If he has the moment to strike, perhaps," Bryn said. "But we dinnae need any man to do our work or bring us pleasure, do we, my sisters?"

Chapter Thirteen

CATRIONA WOKE TO the sound of the endless whistling of the dotterels' morning song from the garden. Spending most of the night tossing and turning had left her feeling even more tired than when she'd gone to bed. She glanced up at the shelves of all the toys Ennis had carved for her, which she still sometimes took down to hold. Each lovingly-whittled wooden figure eerily matched some creature she loved from the island. As a wee lass she would pile them on her bed at night, clutching a hare or a duck as she wept herself to sleep.

On the walls of her room Senga had painted the rolling fields of the glen, framed by oaks and scattered with wildflowers. The colors had faded now, but Catriona still found them a comfort. During those first months her new family had done so much to make her feel at home in this strange place, but wooden animals and painted glens couldn't replace the island.

She would have to forget it, and find contentment here, where she was loved and wanted.

As Catriona stretched, her sensitive breasts pressed against the soft old night dress, and a mild ache welled between her thighs. The reminders of Gavin made her pull a pillow over her hot face. She'd given herself to him willingly, and had discovered pleasures she hadn't known existed. She wouldn't feel shamed over that.

Getting out of her childhood bed and dressing for the day had her finding marks from Gavin's loving all over her fair skin. The little love bites and whisker burn made her sigh as she covered them. She'd carry more than memories with her for the next week. In a strange way she felt almost branded by him, as if the marks would turn into ink and become permanent, even if they were just in her memory.

'Tis done, Catriona thought as she touched a tingling spot on the side of her neck. *I've naught to regret.*

In the front room Ennis and Senga were having their morning meal, and smiled at her as she retrieved a bowl and filled it from the pot of oatmeal on the table.

"I've a new mint blend," Ennis told her as he poured a mug of fragrant brew for her. "With a pinch of honeysuckle and verbena, to give it sweetness."

Catriona took a sip and sighed. "'Tis very good." She met his gaze. "But you neednae dose me with mint. I'm calm now." She picked up her spoon, and idly stirred her oatmeal.

"That's the face you gave us when you brought the neighbor's cow herd into the yard," Senga said. "Two hundred head, milling about you like happy kids as they ate their way through the garden. I reckon that was when we ken what we'd taken on." Her expression softened. "Happily, lass. You've been a joy."

"I didnae know what a garden was,"

Catriona admitted. "You were very patient with me." As they were now, waiting for her to confide in them.

"You look exhausted," Ennis said and frowned. "There's a bruise on your neck, too. Did you have a fall?"

"No, I...I dinnae wish to burden you." She tugged at her collar to cover the spot, and felt her cheeks pinking. "I need work. I wonder if the cows still like me. Mayhap I should go to work at the dairy."

Ennis reached across the table to touch her hand. "You can trust us, Moggy, whatever it might be."

"Aye, I do. 'Tis just...I've been foolish." She could keep it to herself, for they'd only worry more if they knew, but Ennis and Senga were more than family. They were the keepers of all her secrets. "Since last I visited, a man came to build a house on the island. A highlander."

Catriona told them of Gavin, and how she'd tried at first to discourage him from settling on Everbay. How she'd felt when he'd crossed the barrier, and how quickly her feelings had grown from curiosity to longing. The way she had tried to help him learn the ways of the island, and how she had nearly betrayed herself and her secrets to him at the falls.

"I told him naught, but I gave myself to him before I left," she said finally, ducking her head. "I wanted to have just one time to remember." She looked up to see Senga frowning. "I ken 'twas wrong to be with a man unmarried. But I'm no' a bairn anymore. I'm a woman now, and I cannae have a love of my own here nor on the island. I dare no'."

"You love him, then?" the other woman asked.

"If I were free to, aye. I would. I would make him happy again." She cradled her mug between her cold hands. "He works on a fisher, where he has friends. Friends who would talk of me, their Blue Lady." She closed her eyes for a moment. "And Daimh would come for me and finish it."

"So, you left this highlander no' kenning where you'd gone?" Senga said and shook her head. "He'll be driving himself mad now, looking for you. Lass, there's naught crueler than that."

"I didnae mean to hurt him." She looked to Ennis for support. "His heart belongs to another. For him, 'twas but a dalliance."

"If he's as honorable as you've said, I think no'," he said gently. "A man like that wouldnae rest until he found you again. If he's druid kind, and found the portal... Lass, you were a bairn when you came here. Think what might happen if this man did, even by chance."

The thought of Gavin enduring the terror of the first crossing through the portal made her heart skip a beat. Doubtless he would come out fighting, here in a place where no one could defend themselves against such a man.

"You must tell the highlander everything," Senga said firmly. "All of it. Then hear what he'll say, and who has his heart now."

"You could bring him here with you," Ennis suggested before Catriona could reply. "We'd help you both to settle, you ken that. And you'd both be safe from Daimh."

Tears welled up in her eyes. "You'd do that for me?"

"We prayed for a child, but were never blessed until you came out of that hayrick,"

Senga told her. "You're as much our daughter as you are Tavish and Isela's child. Of course we would."

All of her troubles unraveled as she realized it was the perfect solution. "But do I tell him about the portal, and you, or bring him through and then explain?"

"He wouldnae believe you," Ennis said wryly. "Bring him here first. He's a highlander, so 'twill no' all be strange to him."

A raven landed on the sill of the open window by the table, reminding Catriona of what she'd forgotten. "I've a nestling to return to the cliffs, and I would bring back some things from the village that belonged to my family. I'll stay the night, and return on the morrow." She let out a breath, and grinned at her family. "I dinnae ken how to thank you for this."

"Leave his weapons on the island," Senga advised her. "I dinnae fancy facing down a highlander who wields a dirk and cudgel."

GAVIN EMERGED from the brush and held his

torch aloft as he scanned the muddy ground again. The flickering light revealed that the rain at dawn had washed away his own tracks, so he had no hope of finding Catriona's. He had bellowed her name so often his voice had been reduced to a raw rasp.

Where could she be? Had she fallen and knocked herself out? Had he terrified her into leaving? How had she gotten off the island?

It was his own facking fault. If he hadn't fallen asleep under the tree, this wouldn't have happened. He'd have gone after her as soon as he'd realized she wasn't coming back.

Gavin retraced his steps to the falls, and stared down into the churning pool as he went over everything in his head again. Yes, she'd been upset when she'd run out of the cave, and even after she'd calmed down she'd told him she was leaving. That had been the final straw for him, that and the good-bye kiss. He'd snapped, and poured all his frustrations and longings over her. He'd shown her exactly how he'd felt but she'd responded so freely and beautifully.

It couldn't be the sex that had driven her from him. He'd given her the chance to walk away and she hadn't. Everything that had happened after that had been by choice—hers and his.

It was something to do with the damned cave.

He went to the hidden entrance and walked through the cascade that hid it. He shielded the torch with his jacket, trying to preserve the flame. Inside the murky little recess, the torch dimmed then flared, showing him more of the interior than he'd seen. He saw a small pallet with old linens and blankets, and the scratched stick-figures on the walls.

She must have hidden in here before, when her uncle had chased her. The thought of Catriona as a little girl, concealing herself here long enough to nearly starve, made his stomach turn.

Tired and heartsick, he sat down and leaned back against the wall. This was where she'd slept, he guessed, on the pallet huddled under a wool blanket. She couldn't have been very old to fit, perhaps a young child. The math began to add up in his head. Catriona looked to be in her mid- to late-twenties.

Twenty years ago, she would have been a young child.

Twenty years ago, the undead had come to the island and massacred the druid tribe that had lived here.

Something caught Gavin's eye, and he shifted the torch to illuminate the wall beside him. She'd etched another drawing on this wall. It was much larger than the other, and showed the stick figures of her tribe being throttled, bitten and torn apart by other figures with traces of chalk in their lines. Of course, chalk to make the undead figures white. She must have witnessed the massacre and etched it in the stone. Not for her own amusement, but so there would be a record of it. Now he understood the terror that had kept her so isolated and private about her life.

Catriona must have been a member of the tribe that had been wiped out.

Making that connection explained so much Gavin hadn't understood. Her initial fear of him, and the strange accusations she'd made. She'd lived in so much terror that she had been in hiding her entire life. The village in the glen with its protective barrier was just a larger version of the falls cave. He'd done nothing since coming here but lure her out of the only place she'd felt safe.

Gavin would have slammed his head back against the stone wall, but knocking himself out wouldn't help him find Catriona. He had gone to his cottage, the village and walked the shoreline. He'd searched every inch of the forest around the falls. He needed to be more methodical now. She wouldn't have only two hiding spots on the island. As frightened as she was of being found there would be others. She'd disappeared from the trail to the pool, so he'd follow that, and see if it branched away from the falls. He might find her in another cave in the cliffs.

He had to find her.

The sunrise filtered through the rushing waters, adding dappled light to the cave as he rose to his feet and made his way out. Once outside the cascade, he shook the water from his dripping hair and dragged it back from his eyes.

"Gavin."

The sound of Catriona's voice stunned him so much the torch fell from his grip, and tumbled down to extinguish itself in the frothy pool. She stood only a few yards away from him, wrapped in a soft gray shawl over a spotless blue gown. Her hair flowed over her shoulders like a curtain of auburn satin, and she held two white blooms in her hand.

She looked like such a dream he couldn't stop staring at her. "Where did you go?"

"No' here," she said, her mouth taking on a wry curve. "But I've come back. I'd have been here sooner, but I had to first see to Jester. I've so much to tell you." She held out one of the flowers. "If you wish to listen."

He crossed the distance between them in a handful of strides, and snatched her off her feet. Holding her against him, he buried his face in her hair. "I thought you'd left the island. That I'd finally driven you away forever."

"You cannae do that, my lad." She clutched him tightly, stroking him with her slim, cool hands. "I'll no' keep anything secret from you again."

He drew back enough to look at her face. Though her eyes were underlined with dark circles, she was alive, and beautiful, and his, and that was all that mattered to him. "I'm taking you back to the cottage."

Catriona smiled. "And there?"

"You'll tell me everything." He swung her up into his arms, holding her securely as he made for the trail.

She clasped her hands behind his neck, and sighed as if relieved as he carried her through the forest. Gavin caught the scent of mint and honeysuckle on her breath, and kissed her lips to taste it.

"More of that and we'll no' make it," she whispered.

"Aye." Already he wanted to fling her to the ground and strip her naked and have her over and over again. But he needed to first understand what had happened to her, and why she was so terrified of being found by her uncle.

Inside he set Catriona on her feet by the hearth, and stripped out of his wet clothes. He watched her as he rubbed his damp body dry with a cloth, and her cheeks pinked, but she didn't look away. Once he was dressed he tossed some split logs on the fire, and drew her down to sit with him in front of the hearth.

Cradling her face, he kissed her brow, and then took in her dazzled expression. He didn't want to ruin her delight by questioning her about the past, so he said, "We dinnae have to talk now. 'Tis enough to have you back."

"'Tis time for the truth." She climbed onto his lap, and took his hand in hers. "I was born here on Everbay, to the tribe of the Moon Wake people. They lived as druids do, apart from the mortal islanders, but always willing to help others. My father was a fine fisherman, and my mother a skilled herbalist. 'Twas from them I learned how to net and gather."

He listened as she described her idyllic childhood on the island, and how much she had been loved. Only when she mentioned her father's brother did her expression change.

"My uncle Daimh wasnae content to live on Everbay, so I saw him only rarely. When he did come he often quarreled with the others." Her lips twisted. "I didnae like him, and not only because he angered my father. When he smiled, 'twas too wide, and when he talked, his voice scratched at my ears. Hunger always filled his eyes, and he never stopped moving, like the basker. He felt cold and dangerous to

me, as the sea is where the currents run dark
and hard. He made my mother afraid, and she
feared naught."

Catriona's voice faltered a few times as she
told him of raids on the other islands by the
undead, and the spell barrier the Moon Wake
used to surround and protect their village from
such an attack. By then her uncle had fallen
out with the rest of his tribe over his use of
dark, forbidden magics, and had left the island
vowing never to return.

"His leaving gave no ease to my mother.
Soon after Daimh stopped coming to Everbay
she made me promise to run away if he ever
did. I was to go to the cave under the falls, and
wait there for her. She put food and water and
blankets there for me. Then she said if she
didnae come, I had to leave the island alone."
She took in a deep breath. "One night she
woke me, and bid me run. As I did I looked
back, and saw the barrier fall. My uncle had
returned, and with him hundreds of the
undead. I hid at the edge of the glen and
watched as they killed everyone." Her voice
broke on the last words.

Gavin held her for a long time without

speaking. Then, in a soft voice, he said, "You drew what happened that night on the walls of the cave."

Catriona nodded tightly. "I thought if Daimh found me, then the cave would tell the story. Only he didnae come, and neither did my mother. I waited so long for her, Gavin. I waited until I had naught left to eat, and even then."

Staring at the flames in the hearth, she told him how starvation had finally driven her from the cave. How she'd watched from the forest as strange druids arrived to bury the dead, and place a new barrier around her village.

"The last to go was an old man with the softest eyes. He looked kind, like my father, but my uncle was with him. Daimh pretended to be sad, and wept over the graves. He spoke of loving my parents, and despairing that they had been murdered so cruelly. That was when I understood why my mother had told me to run. My uncle would kill me to hide what he had done. So, I left Everbay." She smiled wanly. "A man named Ennis found me, half-dead in a ditch. He and his wife

Senga took me in, and became my new family."

Caring as they were, living with the very protective mortal couple had still been a painful adjustment, Catriona admitted, and she began making visits to the island in secret. As she grew older she finally entrusted them with the truth of her past.

"They would have me with them always, but they ken that I am no' like them." She sighed. "I've tried to be content there, for coming here is dangerous. If Daimh ever learns I live, I do not know what he will do. Maybe bring the undead back to the island to finish what they started."

Gavin clamped down on the rage billowing inside him. "No' as long as I draw breath, my sweet Cat."

She brushed his mouth with her fingertips. "I ken you will protect me." She closed her eyes. "'Tis the work of the warrior in you."

Gavin thought of everything he still kept secret from her. He wanted to tell her about his time in the service, and what he'd learned while fighting in the Middle East until his disease had forced his discharge from The

Black Watch. But how could he explain to her that he was not just a warrior from the highlands, but the twenty-first century?

The soft purr of her breath told him he didn't have to say anything more now, for Catriona had fallen into a deep sleep. Gently he lifted her and carried her over to his bed, where he stretched out beside her. She turned to cuddle against him, and he pulled his tartan over them. Finally able to relax, he wrapped an arm around her and closed his eyes.

Chapter Fourteen

THAT MORNING CAILEAN finished packing for the journey to Everbay, and studied the contents of his satchel before strapping it closed. He knew not what to expect when they arrived, and the sinking feeling in his belly had only grown worse since dawn. He'd tried to meditate away the despair, but his mind kept toying with the possibilities of what awaited them. They jabbed at his calm like sharp stones, hurled at him from a dark past.

When he emerged from his modest cottage a smiling druidess came to greet him.

"A message for you has just arrived, Ovate Lusk." She offered him a small scroll before she bowed and went on her way.

The small slip contained nothing good, for just the feel of it seemed to burn his fingers. He went back inside before he read the contents, and fell to his knees as Bethany Gordon's frantic plea tore at his soul.

Danyel is gone. Whoever took him killed all of the guards in the family wing last night, and left a Roman word scratched on the wall above his crib. UMQUANSINUM. Please, Cailean, help us find our son.

A knock came on the door of his cottage, and he staggered to his feet to find Lachlan and Kinley McDonnel on his doorstep. Their smiles vanished, and Lachlan reached out to catch him as he reeled backward.

"Forgive me," Cailean gasped. He could hardly form the words, and when he met Kinley's concerned gaze new horror sliced through him. "I've had dreadful news."

"Easy now, lad." The laird helped him inside to a chair, while Kinley fetched a cup of water from his kitchen. He tried to take a sip, but his hand shook so badly he merely spilled half the contents down the front of his robe.

"Should we send for a healer?" Lachlan asked gently.

"No, 'tis only a bad shock." He looked around, his humble room seeming to close in on him now. "The Gordon's son, Danyel, has been stolen from their stronghold. They came for him last night, and killed the guards." He looked up at the laird. "'Twas the undead. They left a Roman word etched into the wall, but why? Why take the boy when they might have the laird, and his lady lay sleeping in the same hall?"

"We'll summon the clan," Lachlan said.

"Diana can track whoever took Danyel," Kinley told him firmly.

Cailean couldn't look at her. "You cannae fathom what this means."

"Do we no'?" Lachlan said. "In a stronghold where of late a druid attends to the lady, she bears a bairn within a year." When Cailean would have denied it all, the laird held up his hand. "We ken Bethany's son wasnae sired by Gordon, for the laird's lover is his bodyguard, no' his wife."

"That, and Danyel has your eyes," Kinley said gently.

Cailean glanced down at the message he still clutched tightly. "My lord, you ken much of the Roman language. Danyel Gordon is an innocent bairn. Do what you will to me, but please." He held out the scroll. "Please help me find my son."

The laird took it and read the message. "This word left on the wall isnae one. It is two, run together. Apart they mean *always*, and *cove*." His mouth tightened. "'Tis how they would write 'Everbay.'"

Cailean felt his fear expand a hundredfold. "We must speak to Master Flen at once."

Chapter Fifteen

WHEN GAVIN OPENED his eyes again the cottage had gone dark. Easing off the bed, he went to build the fire, and then went outside to relieve his bladder. From the position of the moon he knew it was near midnight. They'd slept through the entire day and half the night. When he returned inside he saw his bed was empty, but Catriona's gown lay beside it. The tartan and his lady had gone out the back door into the woods, likely so she might answer the same call of nature.

He stripped out of his tunic, washed out his mouth with some whiskey, and then found some ripe sand pears that would serve as a midnight snack. He was considering making a brew when Catriona slipped back inside, wrapped up in his tartan and nibbling on a sorrel leaf.

The firelight danced in the red tones of her hair, making her tousled mane look as if it had been strewn with tiny garnets. She'd draped the old blue tartan around herself like the gown of a goddess, and it wrapped around her slender body like the finest of silks. It struck Gavin then, just how beautiful she was —and completely unconscious of it as well.

"I would have hunted for berries, but 'tis too dark." She came to him, the scent of the sorrel perfuming her like tart strawberry, and let the tartan slide a little from her bare shoulder. "And then I left my gown and clogs here. 'Twould no' be wise to scamper about the forest wearing only your plaid."

"About that." He tugged at the fold over her breasts. "'Tis a cold night. I'll want it back."

She pouted a little. "How shall I keep warm?"

Gavin grinned. "I ken a man who can help

you with that." Just as he made to take her in
his arms, she sidled away from him. "He's very
good, Cat."

"Och, right, for I've met him," she said
gravely as she stole one of his pears and
nibbled at it. "He kept me warm on the shore
one night, as proper as you like, save for one
kiss that fair curled my toes." She eyed him.
"I'd have the other. That great, grand beast of
a man who seizes me and touches me and
doesnae stop with one kiss, even in the
pouring rain. Can you persuade him to
warm me?"

"That beast is no' very good," Gavin
warned as he went to her, and threaded his
fingers through her hair to tip back her head.
"He wants only to have you naked, under him
in his bed, where he can have his way with
you." Her eyes had gone dark, and her lips
glistened with the juice from the pear. The
combination made his blood burn. "I
wouldnae tempt him."

"But he makes me feel such things." She
moved her shoulders, loosening the tartan,
and watched his face as it slipped down. "He's

only to look at me and I grow hot and restless. And see now." She let the tartan fall to her waist, baring her red, tightly-puckered nipples. "What he does to my body."

Their first time together had been so passionate and emotionally-charged that Gavin had lost complete control. Now she was offering herself to him again, teasing and playful, with complete trust and openness. He didn't deserve her, but he'd spend the rest of his days trying to.

"I'm your man, then."

He stepped back to strip off his trews, and reached to push the tartan over her hips, letting it fall to the floor. Drawing her closer, he ran his hands from her shoulders to the tight, delicious curves of her buttocks. She wriggled against him as he clamped hold and lifted her, his cock pressing into her belly like a twitching iron rod.

A sigh of longing stuttered out of her. "Do you never do this in a bed, my fine beast?"

The last woman he had taken to bed had been Thora, but the memory no longer made him feel miserable. He had started his life over, and Catriona, who was as honest and loving as

Thora had been deceitful and full of hate, would never betray him.

"Mayhap you should teach me that, too," he told her, walking with her plastered against his chest to drop with her on the bed. "How do we begin, my sweet Cat?"

"You must do as I show you." She climbed over him, straddling his belly as she pushed him back against the ticking. "Close your eyes, and dinnae peek."

Gavin obeyed her, although he grumbled over being denied the sight of her lovely, flushed face and pretty, tight-peaked breasts. She lifted up, shifting down to graze his cock with the damp softness between her thighs, before she settled on his legs. Her hands swept over his chest, stroking his muscles with tantalizing caresses. The brush of her hair joined her fingers as she put her mouth in the space between his collarbones, and used her tongue there to trace the hollow.

The touch of her lips made his shaft swell, and then he felt an odd, sharp sensation spread over his upper arm. "What do you now to me, sweet Cat?"

"I mean to cover you with kisses," she

murmured as she moved her lips to the flat pebbles of his masculine nipples, laving one and then the other. "That makes you shake."

"You make me crazed." Gavin almost opened his eyes as he felt the needling sensation in his bicep grow more intense. "Do you use your nails on me?"

She murmured a no before sliding down to his belly, where she tongued his navel and circled it with kisses.

"I'm here." The soft curve of her cheek rubbed against the throbbing swell of his shaft. "You'll want to look now, I ken, but– *Gods, Gavin.*"

Light filled his eyes as he opened them, and saw a gilded blue haze. He dragged Catriona up onto him, holding her as power surged through his body. He felt something clawing at his arm now, and turned his head to see the inked lion staring back as it crouched, as if to spring.

"Lovely Cat." The words came out of his mouth in a low, feral growl of a voice that was nothing like his own. "I've lain in wait for you, watching and wanting. Give yourself to me, and I shall make you my queen."

She should have shoved herself away and fled, but Catriona only stared back at the lion. She reached for his arm, and ran her fingertips over the ink as if to stroke the bristling back. "The beast awakes in you."

Gavin struggled with the power, fighting for control. "Cat, get away from me before it hurts—"

"'Twill no' harm me," she whispered. "'Tis part of you. I can feel him now. He wants us both. He wants to share our pleasure."

A rumbling groan erupted from Gavin as he rolled Catriona under him, pinning her beneath his weight. His cock felt as if it might explode before he could get inside her, but still he tried to be gentle as he fitted his straining dome to the wet ellipse of her opening.

She arched under him. "Dinnae keep it from me, please, Gavin, please. I need you."

۞

SEEING Gavin's skinwork come alive with light had been startling, even a little frightening, but as soon as Catriona sensed the presence of the beast his purpose flooded her. He had slumbered deep within the highlander until Gavin had come to the island. What they had shared at the falls had roused him from his sleep, and now he wanted everything.

From the rigid set of his shoulders Gavin still resisted the beast, but she could feel his will wavering. Deliberately she stroked his ink again, this time with the edge of her nails, and spread her thighs wider. Her folds splayed over his swollen dome, drenching him with her silkiness as she lifted her hips.

"There," she whispered, tugging his head down to hers as she moved against him. "'Tis where you belong. Inside me, loving me. You cannae hurt me when I want you so much. Give me all of you, my man, my beast."

Gavin's body jerked over her as he penetrated her with a slow, heavy thrust, his shaft stretching her as it plunged in. He drew back to watch her face, his own tight with hunger, and plowed as deeply as she could take him. Once planted in her, he swelled even more, his cock filling her as if their sexes had locked together. Then he moved, drawing back to thrust again, and it still felt as if he were inside her, stretching her to her limits.

"You are his mate and mine, my naked Queen," the spirit's voice said, rumbling. "I possess you with him."

"Aye, we do." Gavin watched her face as he worked in and out of her with steady, passionate strokes. "Give me your lips now. I want to taste your cries as I fack you."

Catriona pressed her mouth to his just as a moan erupted, and he drank it from her, his hands dragging her legs up around him, his tongue sliding deep. Her breasts heaved against his chest, hot and aching, and the rasp of her nipples on his skin drew his mouth from hers.

His breath rushed against her ear as he muttered, "I want to mark you with my mouth and my hands and my seed. I want you to wear me like another skin. You'll never be free of me, my beautiful Catriona."

His words hurled her past pleasure and into a dark, hot explosion of bliss that stretched on and on until she cried out his name, and he took her mouth again.

Catriona clung to him, kissing him back as her body writhed under his. Still he pumped in and out of her, riding her delight until he dragged her from the trembling end into yet another release. All she knew was him and his devouring mouth and his hard, endless facking.

When his eruption came he drove into her and held himself deep, ending the kiss to fling his head back and let loose the roar of the beast. Inside her body his cock and that of the spirit's pumped together, saturating her with creamy heat and soft, satisfied power. It spread through her like light, rushing into her womb and curling there to resonate with the purr of an exultant feline.

Deep inside her Catriona felt a glow begin, unlike any she had ever known.

Gavin collapsed, his big frame shaking, and rolled onto his back with her still impaled on him. He held her there, brushing the hair from her face and caressing her spine as they both trembled through the aftershocks.

His hand abruptly stilled, and he lifted her from him to put her on her side. He checked her from her lips to her thighs, his fingertips searching for she knew not what. Only when he touched her belly did she feel a tenderness that made her glance down.

Just above her navel a shape like a lion's paw appeared, etched in gold and blue as if she had been inked.

"You marked me." She gingerly touched the skinwork, which sent a pleasant tingle through her fingers, and then she saw his expression. "It doesnae hurt. 'Tis just a surprise and a very pretty one." It wasn't what was causing the glowing sensation, however.

"I didnae do this." He bent his head to examine the ink more closely, and then checked his shoulder. "'Tis the same as mine, but how?"

A dim memory came back to her, and she almost cried out as she realized what the glow was, but she couldn't tell him that now. He would think her crazed for certain.

Quickly she focused on his ink, and recalled where she had seen it before this night. "Men with skinwork like yours came to Everbay once. I dinnae ken why, but my mother said they were Pritani."

Gavin's expression turned grim. "Likely they came hunting the undead."

"I wish I might tell you more of them, but they didnae stay long." She caressed his ink with gentle fingers. "I'm glad you marked me. I like your beast very much."

He gathered her close. "Even when I've told you naught of my life," he said gruffly, "Nor my past?"

"You will when 'tis time for me to ken." As she would, once they left the island.

"But I do have a confession," he said, his eyes looking deeply into hers.

Her excitement dimmed. "Out with it."

"The Mollers didnae take the fisher to Shetland," he said, as a grin spread across his face. "'Tis a slow time since the herring have no' yet begun to run, so Bjarke granted my want for leave."

She traced the curved line of his mouth. "I've still something to tell you too, but I must first take you to meet Ennis and Senga."

Gavin nodded. "And where do they live?"

She allowed herself a small, smug smile. "I'll take you there in the morning. I've told them a little about us, and they are eager to meet you. No, dinnae scowl so. They're the best and kindest of folk." Her gaze shifted to the window, and what she saw there gave her a start. "Gods above. 'Tis dawn now." She frowned at him. "Where went the night?"

He gave her a tender kiss. "I didnae notice. You kept me busy, wench."

"Expect many nights the same." Catriona rose to her feet, tugging him up. "Come outside, and watch the sunrise with me."

He wrapped her in his tartan before he pulled on his trews and followed her through the door. The grass bowed, heavy with dew, and the air had the clear, cool scent of night rain. She walked with him into the clear, where she saw a perfect rainbow arcing over the island. It stretched across the pale sky with bands so vivid they seemed painted.

Her hand crept to cover the tiny glow in her belly as she turned to him. "'Tis an omen to see a full rainbow at dawn. It means that a great circle will soon be completed. What was will return to what is."

Gavin smiled and put his arm around her. "You've come back to me, so I believe it."

She saw the beauty of the colors reflected

in his moonstone eyes, and knew in that moment she would love him for the rest of her days. "You'll no' have to chase me again, my lad."

Chapter Sixteen

PREPARING FOR HIS journey to Everbay took Daimh most of the day. Once he had struck the bargain with Quintus Seneca, the tribune who now ruled over the undead, he waited to be sure the Gordon lad was abducted. While he felt sure Seneca would keep his word, he would not rely on it. He privately arranged for his passage, attended to the rituals necessary to strengthen his body wards, and kept close watch on Cailean Lusk and Bhaltair Flen as well. When Cailean advised him that the laird and his lady would arrive the next morning to make the jaunt to the island, he finished the last of his schemes.

At dawn Daimh went to peer in the

window of Bhaltair Flen's house. The old druid lay unmoving where he had fallen by his table, his half-eaten dinner congealed on his plate. Sensing no one else in the place, Daimh slipped inside.

"Brother Bhaltair." He crouched down beside the man, taking care not to step in the puddle of spew by the old man's mouth. "Can you hear me? Are you sick?" He prodded the old druid's shoulder, and then grabbed a handful of his silver hair to lift up his head. "'Twould seem that you are. 'Tis never wise to drink from poisoned goblets."

Daimh released Bhaltair's head, smiling as it thunked on the floor boards. The old fool never thought to secure his doors, more the pity for him. Nimbly he went to the table to remove the goblet he'd stolen and coated with a very unpleasant potion before returning it. Taking it to the kitchen, he washed it thoroughly before filling it halfway with perry and placing it back by the unfinished meal.

"When you awake you'll wish you were dead, but 'twill likely no' kill you," Daimh said as he surveyed the tableau. "I might have ended you, but you're worth more to me alive.

Either way, I cannae have one as powerful as you with us on Everbay, you see."

Daimh went to the window, and saw the McDonnel laird, his lady and Ovate Lusk making their way toward Bhaltair's door. Quickly he left the old druid's house through the back, hurrying into the woods beyond it. By the time he reached the horse he'd hidden his heart pounded in his ears and he had to rest until he caught his breath. A hiss came from the tightly-secured pack on the horse's rump, and it shook a few times.

"Patience, Anoup." With some difficulty he mounted the gelding, and reached back to give the pack a fond pat. "We'll be on our way now."

One of the few disadvantages to embracing dark magics was Daimh's inability to use sacred oak portals for travel. The cursed trees no longer recognized him as druid, and refused to transport him. As he rode to the coast, he ignored the discomforts the horse's quick pace caused him. Once he transcended, his physical ailments would vanish, and the powers bestowed on him by the dark god Anubis would be unlimited. He'd never again be obliged to plod about like a mortal, or bow before the arses of the druid conclave.

Once in town Daimh left his mount at a public stable and made his way to the docks. There he found the two free traders he had paid to sail him out for his rendezvous with the black ship. Both were known cutthroats who would slice their sires for the right price.

"Coin first," the dirtier of the pair demanded, and scowled as soon as he checked inside the purse Daimh handed him. "'Tis no' enough."

"'Tis half your fee," he told him. "You'll have the rest once we reach the ship." Seeing the other man's snarling expression, he added, "Come, man. You ken to whom I go. If you dinnae fear the wrath of the undead, then leave me here. You willnae regret it until after the sun sets, when they come for you."

That threat wiped the resentment from the smugglers' faces, replacing it with craven fear. The first pocketed the purse before jabbing his finger at a decrepit-looking fisher with a rein-forced hull and nets and traps disguising its hidden cargo niches.

Daimh sat at the front of the boat to enjoy

the rush of the wind as they sailed west from the docks. Land-locked as he had been for the last twenty years, he had missed the cold saltiness of the sea air. He had already decided that once he'd finished the ritual he would build his stronghold on Everbay.

Returning to his old home would bring back unfortunate memories, of course. The endless bickering with Tavish, who had been as short-sighted as he had been undeserving. Isela's lovely face and solemn eyes, ever watching him. He knew she'd chosen his brother over him because Tavish had filled her head with lies. For years he'd pretended to accept their bonding. He'd even celebrated the birth of their brat.

He'd waylaid Isela on his last visit to the island, catching her as she walked back from gathering in the woods. He'd offered her his heart and every comfort and luxury she could wish for, if only she would admit her mistake in choosing the wrong Haral, and come away with him.

I've sensed how you want me, Brother, she'd said at last. *But I've never encouraged you by look, word or deed. There is a darkness in you that soon shall grow beyond any hope of redemption. If you dinnae turn from your path, 'twill be the ruin of you.*

Then turn me, my love, Daimh had begged. *For I cannae go on without you.*

She'd smiled sadly. *You lie to yourself now, Brother. My heart belongs to my husband and our daughter. You may lust for me, but you love only power.*

Such had been his disappointment that Daimh had struck her, hard enough to knock her to the ground, and then raged over her. *Do you no' ken who I am? What I will become? I can give you everything.*

She had wiped the blood from her mouth on the back of her hand as she got to her feet, and new wariness had darkened her eyes. *May the gods forgive you.* She'd continued on to the village, never once looking back at him.

The unspoken words she left in her wake had taunted him: *For never shall I.*

His lovely Isela had decided the fate of the Moon Wake tribe that night. He'd thought back on her refusal when he'd found the Anubis ritual scroll. Once he'd deciphered its meaning, he'd known how he would take revenge against his tribe. He'd risked his life to strike that first bargain with the undead, but it had been worth it. It had felt so good to see the look on his brother's face when Daimh had dispelled the barrier and marched in with his monstrous army. He'd watched the undead bathe in the blood and flesh of every weak, mewling druid on the island. Daimh had intended to violate Isela personally, but the Romans had found her dead beside his brother, with the blades they had used still buried in their hearts.

Their suicides had distracted him from looking for their brat. Indeed, once the undead left and the sun rose, the carnage left behind was such that Daimh hardly recognized any of the bodies. He'd never expected his niece of seven years to successfully elude the Ninth Legion. When the Anubis ritual had failed to change him, he had gone on a rampage, searching every inch of the island for any survivors, and finding nothing but more corpses. He had doubted the dark magic —and himself—when he should have known Isela's facking brat was responsible.

The black ship appeared on the horizon some hours later, and anchored as the free traders' boat approached it. Daimh slipped on gloves made on bespelled hide, retrieved his pack, and soothed Anoup's agitation by patting the side.

"'Tis come for ye," the filthier smuggler said and planted himself in front of Daimh, and brandished an impressive-looking dagger. "We'll be having our due. Now."

"Of course." Daimh smiled cheerfully as he reached into the outer pouch of his pack.

The smuggler snatched away the large stack of coins he produced, and shoved them in the hands of his partner. "Drop the rest," he ordered, emphasizing his intent with a jab of the blade toward Daimh's belly. "Then get the fack off our boat."

It always paid to hire the untrustworthy, Daimh thought as he gently placed the pack on the deck between them. They were so incessantly predictable. For a moment he considered opening the flap to show the idiot the deadly contents. But touching the coins with their bare hands had already put the curse to work. The large blade and the rest of Daimh's payment clattered to the deck as both men howled and clawed at their blackening hands.

"Do give my best to the great god Sekhmet," he told the smugglers as they both collapsed, writhing and frothing at the mouth. He chuckled as he retrieved his pack. "'Twill cheer her as she takes you to be slaughtered by her demon butchers."

No stranger to boats, Daimh guided the fisher the rest of the way to come alongside the black ship, and stepped off onto the rope ladder. Two mortal crewmen helped him onto the deck, and one made as if to take his case.

"No, lad," he told him before he made his way to the stern-faced man at the helm. "You may weigh anchor and continue on now, Captain."

The man shouted the order as Daimh returned to the railing, and glanced down to see the two piles of black ooze that was all that remained of the smugglers. Daimh never left behind any witnesses to his dark endeavors, and anyone who found the boat would think it abandoned.

The tribune had not named the place they were to rendezvous, but some hours later Daimh recognized it as they approached the Isle of Staffa.

Daimh marveled at the new tribune's ingenious solution to safeguarding the undead. In his memory no mortals had ever settled on the small island, which offered little in the way of soil for crop-growing. Ships also gave the place a wide berth, as Staffa's strong resemblance to a half-sunken giant's temple made sailors uneasy.

It made an ideal haven for the blood-drinkers, however. The enormous sea caves offered complete protection from the sun's rays, and he felt certain that the Romans had tunneled their way even deeper into the rock beneath the surface to create their lair. The legion's black ships sailed mostly at night, and ran without lights, rendering them virtually invisible on the seas.

Daimh felt as excited as a lad at his first ritual. When Cailean and the McDonnels found Bhaltair poisoned, they would go in search of him to assure he had not been harmed. Then they would find the note he had left in his house. Leaving word that he would meet them on the island that evening had been a particularly masterful touch. Thinking Daimh had gone straight into the arms of the legion there would spur them to make the jaunt at once. Believing his son in the hands of the undead, Cailean would depend on the laird to take charge. Once Daimh had both men on the island he would bring the legion and the boy. The lot of them could burn or drown or run. He didn't care as long as that lass—the last member of his tribe —was there.

Never again would he need gulp poppy juice to ease his pain.

The ship slowed as the crew dropped anchor, and the captain came to join Daimh. "My master and his men will board tonight, and then we shall set sail for Everbay."

Chapter Seventeen

✦

GAVIN EXPECTED CATRIONA to take him to the boat she'd been using to travel to the island, but instead of heading for the shore once they were packed she led him down the path to the falls.

"Do you leave from the other side of the cliffs?" he asked once they'd passed the cascade and stopped at a fork in the trail. "And dinnae tell me that you climb them."

She chuckled. "I dinnae have to. Now, you mustnae ask more questions, or 'twill spoil the surprise."

The trek ended with the two of them standing in front of a cliff that towered at least fifteen meters overhead. Gavin caught her arm as she made as if to walk into the rocky face, and then saw half her body vanish from sight.

"Another hidden entrance?" he asked, and when she nodded he gripped her hand and followed her into the narrow gap he hadn't seen. Just inside the entry a heavy curtain of flowered vines covered what lay within.

"Falling vine," Catriona told him as she swept aside the mass. "'Twill grow anywhere, so my tribe planted it to make a door of sorts."

Gavin went with her into the tunnel behind the vines. Judging by its symmetry and the marks left by the excavation work, her people had spent months, maybe years digging through the cliff. Strange symbols had been etched into the walls in two parallel lines, and had been punctuated with spiral shapes sprouting small leaves.

For the first time since he'd come to Everbay he felt uneasy. Where had he seen that image before?

"'Tis just outside the passage," Catriona told him, gesturing to the lighted end of the tunnel. When she glanced at his face she squeezed his hand. "Dinnae worry. I've left and come to the island so many times this way, I cannae count them. I've never once come to harm, I promise."

Gavin nodded, but when they emerged from the passage he didn't see a boat or a shore. A huge grove of trees encircled a wide clearing, the center of which had been decorated with carved stones. The carvings appeared to be smaller renderings of the symbols from the tunnel, and each had been topped with a leafy spiral.

He felt a tug in his chest as he stared at the very center of the place, a pull that felt almost pleasant, as if he were wanted.

Catriona stopped at the edge of the clearing. "My tribe planted oaks here to grow and protect the place from the shore. Only through the passage can it be reached now." A flicker of worry passed over her pretty face. "Do you trust me, Gavin? I cannae take you with me unless you do."

"Aye, but I dinnae see how we may leave Everbay." He glanced around. "Do you perform a spell here to fly away to another island?"

"No, lad, 'tis all done by the gods. They've

made open the door. We've only to take a few more steps to go through it." She pulled on his hand, urging him into the clearing.

Every step Gavin took felt heavier and slower, and the tug in his chest became a frantic thud. At the same time his legs didn't stop moving, even when he tried to lock his knees. Whatever was going to happen, he couldn't avoid it now, he thought, his heart hammering as he stepped with her into the center of the stones.

The ground dissolved beneath them, and Gavin plunged into a dark, whirling tunnel of curving, thrashing oaks. He was crossing over again, just as he had when he and Jema had fallen into the pit at her dig in the future. He could hear Catriona laughing, and felt his body stretching and then shrinking, as if he were dwindling away. Pain seeped into his joints, and his muscles locked. Finally, he landed on a hard, grassy surface, his chest sinking under his tunic as he struggled to breathe.

All around him the mountains of the high-lands rose, as ancient and majestic as Gavin remembered them. A tractor blooming with rust sat not two meters away behind a wire fence, which stretched out on either side of a utility pole with a boxy distribution transformer bolted on one side. A shadow passed over him along with a quiet roar as a jumbo jet soared through the clouds above.

They were still in Scotland, but no longer in the fourteenth century.

Catriona took several steps, her arms flinging wide as if she meant to embrace this new world. Her long fiery hair had been shorn away into a delicate pixie cut that spiked all around her head.

He did his best to stumble after her, but only made it a few paces before his spindly legs collapsed beneath him.

"Welcome to my other home, Gavin. 'Twill seem odd to you, but 'tis the same Scotland you ken, just older." She spun around, showing him a slightly different face, with a small scar dividing her right brow, and a light sunburn pinking her cheeks and nose. Under the bangs of her bob haircut, her blue-violet eyes flared wide as she stared in horror at him. "Mr. McShane?"

"Iona," he breathed, finally understanding

why she'd somehow seemed familiar. He took as deep a breath as he could, for if he passed out like this she wouldn't know what to do. "How?"

She shook her head helplessly, and then flung herself down on the ground beside him. "'Tis you. But how can you be... Oh, gods, no."

"The same man. Gavin McShane. You ken." He struggled for more air, hating the way he had to gasp out his words. "I dinnae have...ALS in your time."

She went so white her sunburn looked blazing red now. "You're a traveler, like me."

"Crossing over healed me." Spasms racked his legs, and he gritted his teeth. "Coming back did the opposite."

Two middle-aged people in modern clothing appeared behind her. One Gavin recognized as Ennis, Iona's father and the head gardener at his family's old estate. They had to be the couple she'd told him about that had taken her in—when she'd crossed over from the past, he now realized.

"Master McShane," Ennis said, his eyes wide. He turned to Iona. "Moggy, how is he

here? He vanished with his sister a
year ago."

"Aye," Senga said flatly. "And now he's
back, and he can't breathe."

Catriona seized Gavin's hand as tears
rolled down her cheeks. "Never did I dream…
Oh, gods, Gavin, what have I done to you?"

"You've brought him for a visit," Senga
said as she lowered herself beside Gavin and
propped him up with her arm. "'Twill be a
short one."

Catriona hadn't told him she'd come from
the future for the same reasons he hadn't
admitted the same, Gavin thought, wanting to
laugh over the irony.

"'Tis why you didnae ken so much on Everbay," Catriona said. "Why you'd never caught
sandies or made baskets or ken the basker
wouldnae harm us. You never learned it."

"I couldn't tell you. I believed you would
have thought me mad." It depressed him to
hear the modern English coming out of his
mouth. "You were a fine teacher, Iona."

"And your sister?" Senga asked.

"Aye," he said, trying to keep his voice

from trembling. "We traveled back together but…we were separated."

"I'd never dreamed you were that poor man in the window," Catriona said.

"She watched for you every time I went to the estate," Ennis said.

"Even when I could sneak in the house," Catriona said, "the maids never let me come close enough to see your eyes."

"I never suspected that the pretty lass who brought lavender for my room was my island beauty." He gulped some air and managed to lace his fingers through hers. "Some days all I had to hold onto was watching you work in the gardens."

"Cat has told us crossing over heals all of her wounds," Senga said. She tapped her eyebrow in the same spot as his lover's scar. "Once there I reckon you'll go back to being a great strapping highlander." Sympathy filled her eyes. "And I fear you cannae be that here, Mr. McShane."

"Oh, aye," Catriona said as she sat up. "On Everbay you'll be well and whole again." As quickly as she had become elated, her face fell and her shoulders slumped. "Only there is Uncle, and if he finds us—"

"He willnae touch you," Gavin promised her even as pain lanced through his legs. "In your time I can protect you." He looked at Ennis and Senga. "You've my word on it."

"That's what I wished to hear," the older woman assured him.

"Daimh is dangerous to more than the two of you," Ennis said. "I've thought a great deal on it since she came to us as a wee lass. Cat told us her uncle was made to leave the tribe because of his use of dark magics. Mayhap he planned the massacre as part of some evil ritual. A man capable of killing all of his kin is a monster."

"One who should be brought to justice," Senga said, and regarded Catriona. "I ken how your uncle frightens you, lass. He murdered your family and took your people from you. But think on it. What if he tried to do the same again to others?"

Catriona's mouth went tight. "'Tis been twenty years, and still I've nightmares. I wouldnae wish it on anyone."

"Nor I," Senga said. "For I've held you

every night here that you've woken scream-
ing." The older woman kissed her brow. "With
Gavin to protect you in your time, you can go
to those in authority, and tell them what you
witnessed. Daimh will be made to answer for
what he did."

Gavin saw the fear that tightened Catriona's expression, and expected her to refuse.
She surprised him again when she said, "Aye, I
can, and I will." She smiled at him. "Then we
never have to hide again."

※

THOUGH DAIMH WOULD LIKE to have seen the
legion's lair on the Isle of Staffa, the captain
had informed him that his orders were that
the druid would remain aboard the black ship.
Though disappointed at first, the older man
found other ways to occupy the day until the
tribune and his men could board that night.
In the brief time he'd been on deck, the
furtive glances of the crew had not gone
unnoticed.

Daimh lingered on the companionway,
just below the quarterdeck. Above him the

sound of clanging metal and boots hurrying back and forth drifted down.

"Swords here and cudgels there," said one rough voice. "Where's the sense in hiding them?"

"'Tis no' for ye to ken," said another man, sounding tired but irritated. "'Tis orders of Prefect Strabo."

As the footsteps stopped, Daimh heard the clatter of weapons being dropped, followed by a loud thump.

"Och, that one with but half a face," said the first man, as the footsteps resumed and crossed back the way they'd come.

"Cap'ns orders too," said the tired voice.

"Look lively there!" said a third voice, cutting off more conversation. "Quit your dawdling!" The two sets of footsteps hurried off.

By Daimh's count, that had been the third trip.

He sat down on the ladder, easing his aching joints, but smiled to himself. It didn't take scrying or spellwork to hear that the tribune had a fair amount of trouble on his hands.

Chapter Eighteen

KINLEY CAME OUT of Bhaltair's bed chamber, and gestured for Lachlan and Cailean to join her in the front room. Other druids waiting there had joined hands and were murmuring invocations to the gods, so she led her husband and the ovate outside.

"The healer says if he survives the night, he'll live." She wrapped her arms around herself. "Which sucks, but at least he's got a chance."

"I've sent word around the settlement about my master's sickness," Cailean told her. "Did the healer say what ails him?"

"It's not any sickness she recognizes." Kinley glanced back at the cottage. "The vomiting is similar to food poisoning, but she said that takes some time to set in. Bhaltair went down *while* he was eating."

Lachlan's nostrils flared. "Deliberately poisoned."

Cailean rubbed his brow. "But I checked everything in the house. There's naught that could have done this." He dropped his hand. "And why? Bhaltair is much-loved and respected. No one would…" He stopped and stared at Kinley. "Never would he take his own life. He's happier now than he has ever been in my memory."

"That old man knows more ways to die quickly than I do," Kinley told him bluntly. "If he wanted to go, he wouldn't have picked this route." She regarded her husband. "We need to send for Diana. She used to process crime scenes. She'll know what to look for."

"Aye, but she'll no' rest until she tears the settlement apart looking for the poisoner," the laird said. "I think 'twill have to be us to do this, Wife."

"All right," Kinley said and walked around for a moment. "This Daimh Haral guy left for Everbay this morning. Then we find Bhaltair half-dead on the floor. Diana would not think that was a coincidence. Let's go have another look at his last meal."

They returned inside and went to the table, where the food and half-filled goblet still sat. The wilted greens and congealed stew looked all right to Kinley, but since any hope of a forensics lab lay seven hundred years away, she turned to Cailean.

"Is this what he usually has for dinner?" When the ovate nodded she picked up the goblet and sniffed it. "Okay, this definitely has alcohol in it. Maybe he just drank too much too fast."

"'Tis called perry," Lachlan told her. "Fermented pear juice, only just more potent than ale. Master Flen isnae a small man. 'Twould take a cask of it to sicken him."

Cailean took the goblet from her. "No, it cannae be perry." After he sniffed it he groaned. "'Twas in the water."

"Now you've lost me," Kinley advised him.

"My master only has water with his evening meal," the ovate said as he set the goblet down. "Anything more gives him the headache and a restless night. He would never touch perry after sunset." He tried to smile. "Indeed, he keeps a jug for me."

"So, the bastard doused his water, dumped it, washed the goblet and refilled it with perry." Kinley slowly walked around the table. "He knew we'd find the old guy, but he didn't give him enough to kill him. He also didn't want us to know he used poison. What's his game?"

"'Tis a delay tactic," Lachlan said. "We intended Bhaltair to come with us. Finding him near death prevented that, and our own departure. He wished to reach the island before us."

Kinley nodded. "As Diana would say, I'm liking Daimh Haral for this." She saw Cailean grimace. "And you really don't like this guy at all. Your lip does the curl thing every time you say his name. Why does he get on your nerves?"

"My own feelings dinnae matter." The young druid gripped the back of his master's chair. "'Tis no' the druid way to harbor ill feelings toward others, and certainly as the last survivor of the Moon Wake tribe, he deserves to be pitied. And yet…"

Kinley rolled her hand.

"Something about him grates on me." Cailean looked to the laird. "When the conclave sent me to Everbay to attend to the tribe's remains, he came. He wept and wailed about his great loss, and 'twas very convincing. Yet when it came to do the work, he offered no aid to me or the other brothers. He stood back and said naught and simply watched."

Kinley thought of the one McDonnel funeral she had seen, where every member of the clan had come forward to pay their respects to Seoc Talorc. The McDonnels had touched the body and spoken of the dead man with affection and respect. Not one of them had stood back and simply watched.

"Did he cry when you put them in the ground, or after, when he was with you?" Kinley asked.

"After," Cailean said, sounding stricken. "After and always, with us."

"Then 'twas a performance, done for your benefit." Lachlan put a hand on the druid's shoulder. "I ken druid kind rely on magics and learning to deal with such things. All of that 'tis beyond me, but I ken betrayal only too well. You were the last druid to attend to Ever-bay. Your son, now stolen to be taken there. Daimh Haral, gone there as Bhaltair is struck down."

Kinley stared at him. "Why would this be about Cailean?"

"I think I ken, but I must be sure." The young druid took in a deep breath, and straightened. "I dinnae wish to leave my master in such a state, but we must go to Ever-bay. This very moment."

Lachlan retrieved his weapons and their packs from their horses while Kinley went with Cailean to fetch his pack. She knew he was blaming himself—he could barely look at her—but that wasn't her main concern.

She waited to ask him as they were walking to meet Lachlan at the settlement's sacred grove. "Do you know why the undead took your son?"

Cailean stumbled, nearly falling over, and then took her offered hand. "Danyel is the last of my bloodline," he said, his voice tight with worry. "Bethany hasnae yet conceived again." He gave her a sheepish look. "We have been trying for another bairn."

"Good for you guys." She wasn't going to judge a woman who had married a gay man with his boyfriend living in the house with them. "So you're worried Bethany won't have any more children."

He looked away from her again. "I think if Danyel dies, 'twill kill her as well."

By then they were at the grove, where Lachlan stood waiting. Another druid, one Kinley recognized as a member of the conclave, stood talking with him. The older druid bowed to her and Cailean before he hurried away.

"What was that about?" she asked her husband.

"I made inquiry as to when Daimh used the portal to travel to Everbay this morning. The conclavist tells me he hasnae." The laird eyed Cailean. "In fact, no' once since he came to live here has Daimh used the grove."

Kinley felt perplexed now. "Why would he avoid using the portal. It works for anyone who has druid blood. No other form of travel in this time is faster. If he wanted to get to Everbay before us, no way is he riding a horse to the nearest dock."

"Unless he had to meet a ship," her husband said. "Mayhap he is in league with the undead now."

"Or he is no longer a druid," Cailean said slowly. "Bhaltair told me once that Daimh doesnae participate in the rituals held here. He claims that he doesnae out of respect for his tribe, but there have been whispers about it. Some say he willnae because it would reveal what he truly is."

"What's that?" Kinley asked.

"One who follows the dark path," he told her. "Worship of gods from other lands, those that demand sacrifices of blood. Magics forbidden to us because they are evil, or destructive. 'Twould explain why Daimh wears body wards. He says 'tis to protect him against the undead, but it blocks any from sensing his magics and powers. If he does such evil things, then it would change him. We would ken that he was no longer one of us."

Chapter Nineteen

JEMA WIPED THE sweat from her brow and leaned back from the pit. The excavation of the Late Bronze Age site had yielded several exciting finds, including a gold-decorated bronze spearhead, a bronze sword, scabbard fittings, and a ruby pin. It was quite the haul, especially considering her excavation tools weren't all that much more modern.

But as she often did at the edge of the pit, her thoughts went back to Gavin and how they'd found their way to fourteenth-century Scotland. Despite knowing that he'd died on that wretched island, her dreams of him seemed so vivid that she often found herself believing he was still alive—until today. She touched her chest as she looked down into the rectangular pit. For the first time in her life, she felt he was gone. Truly gone.

"Here's your empties," Tormod said. Jema blinked away her thoughts as he set down two dirt-caked baskets next to her. "Those mounds of dirt I'm making will soon make fine fortifications."

Jema smiled up at her Viking, stripped to the waist, his glorious body covered in grime and sweat. With the sun behind him, his golden hair shone white.

"We're saving that dirt," she said for possibly the third time. "We'll use it to backfill the excavation pits."

He crouched down beside her, frowning at her forehead. Before she could stop him, he'd licked his thumb and rubbed it just below her hairline.

"You're filthy, wife," he said, smiling at her.

"Don't look now," she said, "but you could use a dip in the stream."

"Aye," he said, cupping the side of her face. "'Twould make two of us. Dinnae tempt me."

Not long after she'd first arrived, Lachlan had given them this lovely bit of land. Along with the circular stone wall, there were several fruit trees, a small orchard, and a stream at the back of the glade. But when Jema glanced in that direction, any thoughts of romping in the water with her Viking vanished.

"Raen?" she said. "And Diana?"

Tormod stood as they emerged from the stream. "This cannae be good."

Still soaking wet, Diana marched directly at him, eating up ground with her long-legged stride. Jema stood as well and took her husband's hand. Behind the tall redhead, Raen looked grim.

"Gods, Red," Tormod said, when she came to a stop in front of him. "You're giving me a fright. Tell me what 'tis?"

But rather than reply to him, Diana faced Jema. "There's word of your brother."

"What?" Jema gasped and felt the world reeling. Tormod wound his arm around her waist and she gratefully leaned on him. "Of Gavin?"

Raen nodded. "'Tis some hidden druid

matter, and there's naught of any certainty, but the laird would not keep it from you."

"After all this time," Tormod said, hugging Jema to his side. "'Tis happy news I hope."

But Jema could see from the faces of their friends that it was not.

"What's happened?" she demanded.

Chapter Twenty

❦

"*OU* ARE HARAL?" Quintus took in the insignificant sight of the puny druid standing on the black ship's deck before eyeing Strabo. "I thought such a turncoat would be taller."

His prefect uttered a sour sound. "None of his kind have ever impressed me, Tribune."

"I think you shall appreciate me more after my transformation is complete," the druid said, puffing himself up a bit as if trying to look taller. "'Tis a fascinating ritual, not unlike what you and your men—"

A wail interrupted him. It came from the blanket-wrapped bundle held by one of the guards, drawing all eyes. A small fist emerged from the swaddling and struck the undead soldier in the face. He bared his fangs and hissed an order to be quiet to the boy, who only shrieked louder.

"Take him below and secure him," Strabo said, and stepped in Daimh's path when the druid tried to follow. "You do not touch the child until Lachlan McDonnel has been captured."

"He'll give himself into your hands quite freely, I assure you," the druid said. His close-set eyes darted around the prefect. "We've only to hold a blade to the boy's throat, if Lusk is present and our timing is—"

"Enough of your prattling," Quintus said, already tired of the little man. "Captain, how long will it take to sail to Everbay?"

The mortal bowed low before he answered. "Most of the night and day, Tribune."

"Then have the crew check our compartments to assure they are light-tight." Quintus went to the railing, and saw a lone, plump figure standing on the cliffs above the lair. She appeared to be waving a small cloth.

"Is that your wife or mate, Tribune?" the

druid asked, earning a snort of contempt from Strabo. "She seems very distraught to see you go. The wives of mortal sailors do the same when their husbands go to sea. Since druids dinnae do such work, our females dinnae indulge in hysterics." He stepped closer, and in a lower voice said, "Might we have a word alone? I've gathered some facts from your crew you may find useful."

Though Quintus eyed him, he said, "This way."

He led Daimh into the Captain's cabin, and called in a guard to station just behind the little man. The odd, medicinal scent coming from the druid's robes made him go to the portal and force it open. Through it he saw Bryn again, which should have made him laugh, but the sight of her fluttering her kerchief only made him think of Fenella. His lost love had always accompanied him on every mission. Indeed, she had saved his life once at great risk to her own.

He felt almost sorry for Bryn and her devotion to him. She would only ever be a whore.

"Tribune, I sense a great sadness in you,"

Daimh said, his voice very different from the chittering he had spewed on the deck. "I dinnae wish to add to it, but I've heard troubling talk."

A curious rage filled Quintus. "Tell me or get out."

"Mortals came on dories to bring weapons on board today while you and your men slept," Daimh said. "They were instructed to place these weapons in various places around the ship."

"The Ninth Legion is ever prepared to engage in battle," Quintus told him. "This we do not do with our bare hands. What of it?"

"'Tis only that the crew hid the weapons," the druid said, his tone simpering now. "I cannae fathom why they would be ordered to do so."

Quintus drew his dagger, and strode over to the guard. Before the man could react, he thrust the blade into his chest, reducing him to a pile of ash. He then held the tip directly under Daimh's nose. "Who ordered it?"

The druid did not twitch an eyelash. "I heard the name Strabo invoked, my lord."

Quintus's fist trembled. As much as he would have liked to cut off Daimh's nose, he had no reason to punish him. He also had no intention of personally searching the ship, or in any way allowing Strabo to learn that his plot had been uncovered.

"Who can attest to the truth of your claim?"

"The captain's loyalties belong to your prefect," the druid admitted. "But the other officers might still be yours."

Quintus had no doubt that the navigator would verify every word the friendly little druid had spoken. He had enthralled the mortal last winter after the undead had captured his ship, and as the tribune's creation he could not lie to him.

"What reason have you to curry favor with me?"

"On Everbay you shall find a druidess, my brother's daughter as it happens." He described the female, and then added, "I wish you to capture her. She is protected by a rogue druid, but he is mortal, and should prove no trouble for your men."

"I suppose you then wish me to hand her over to you with the boy," Quintus said.

Daimh's thin mouth curved. "Och, no, my lord. I wish you to kill her, slowly, and by inflicting as much suffering as you may. While I watch."

Chapter Twenty-One

CATRIONA STOOD, STILL shocked at what had become of Gavin, with his sunken chest, withered legs, and mask of pain. But if anything, she was even more determined to make it right in the past—to make everything right.

"You'll need our help with him, lass," Ennis said.

She took hold of the older man's thin hands. "I wish you could come with us."

"Ah, Moggy," Ennis said, folding her in his arms and hugging her tightly. "This village, this time, is our place, as much as the island is yours. You're a woman grown, and you've a life with Gavin now. Only think of us, and we'll be there with you."

She nodded and let him go but didn't look back at the cottage that had been her sanctuary for so long. She didn't want to part with her family for the last time in tears and sorrow.

"You'll be tempted to cross over again to see us," Senga said, from where she sat beside Gavin. "But your man willnae want you to come alone. You ken what may happen to him if he returns again."

Catriona felt sick as she nodded.

"Another crossing would end me," Gavin ground out between clenched teeth.

"Aye, I think it would. So, for your sake and hers, 'tis good-bye for us." Senga made sure Gavin could sit up on his own before she stood. She kissed Catriona on both cheeks and held her for a long moment. "I dinnae ken why I've dreaded this day. You made me a mother, and Ennis a father, and brought such happiness into our lives. Now I send you to find yours with Gavin, and all our love goes with you both. You are strong, and brave, and you will always be in our hearts."

Those words gave Catriona the courage to let go. She offered Gavin both her hands, which he instantly grasped. Ennis propped him under the shoulder on one side, while Senga did the same on the other.

"Only a few steps," Catriona promised Gavin as she walked backwards, leading him.

"I'm with you, Cat," he wheezed as his arms began to shake.

"All right now, hands about my neck." With her help, Gavin managed to cling to her. "You'll have to let go," she whispered to Ennis and Senga. When they did, Gavin's full weight bore down on her. But she was able to drag him the last step as she glanced back at the two people who had saved her. They stood together, smiling. She burned their image into her memory as she smiled bravely in return.

"Here we go," she said.

Gavin dragged in a breath and held on as he shuffled forward with her into the portal.

They fell into the spinning tunnel of oaks, and a cool wind encircled them as Catriona clung to her love. Gavin's body began to change, his hold tightening as his arms and legs filled out with healthy muscle. The shaking stopped, and his chest expanded with deeper, easier breaths. Catriona felt her feet touch the long grass in the center of the island's grove, and looked up to see Gavin's handsome face and clear eyes. Their hair, grown out long and lustrous, flowed and tangled around them.

"Catriona." He lifted her in his strong arms to give her a long, deep kiss. "We made it."

"Aye, we did." To see him fully restored to a great, muscular beast of a man made her laugh with delight. She ran her fingers through his long hair, and then through her own. "We'll need a trim, though. I've scissors back in the village."

"Really. Have you got any good weapons?" a female voice asked.

Catriona jerked around to see a woman who for a moment she mistook for her mother. Beside the stranger also stood a young druid and a huge Pritani warrior dressed like a laird.

Gavin instantly stepped in front of her. "Are you looking for a fight, lady?"

"Why does everyone think that about me? I mean, I know, I was Air Force, but I rescued people. I didn't fight them." The woman turned to the Pritani. "I should get that tattooed somewhere, sweetheart. Maybe on my forehead."

Catriona peeked around Gavin's knotted bicep, and saw the dreamy eyes of the younger man. He looked very much like the old druid who had come to bury her people. Immediately she thought of her uncle and shuddered.

Gavin reached back to take her hand. "Why have you come here?"

The fierce-looking Pritani took a step forward and bowed. "I am Lachlan, Laird of the McDonnel Clan. This is my lady wife, Kinley Chandler McDonnel, and our friend, Ovate Cailean Lusk. You I reckon are Gavin McShane." His gaze shifted to Catriona. "I fear we dinnae ken your name, my lady."

Her lover curled his hands into huge fists. "You've no' answered my question."

"You've no' introduced us to your lady," the laird countered. "As my wife has said, we dinnae seek to fight. We come to rescue a young lad stolen from his family by our enemies, and learn what more has been amiss on this island. Much, I would say from what I see now."

Catriona heard the steel in his voice, but

saw the kindness in his dark eyes. "Gavin, the Pritani are protectors of mortal and druid kind. Permit me speak to him."

"One move toward her," he told the laird, "and you'll get that fight you dinnae want."

Lachlan nodded, and shifted his gaze to Catriona.

"I am Catriona Haral, the last survivor of the Moon Wake tribe." She noted the start her name gave the druid, but continued on. "Twenty years ago, the undead massacred my people. My uncle, Daimh Haral, brought the Romans through the barrier that protected our village. Since that night I've been hiding from him here, and in another time."

Cailean gestured at the portal. "You've used the grove to cross over to the past, to be with your people when they were alive?"

She shook her head. "The portal took me to a village in the highlands in the twenty-first century."

"You've been living in the future?" Cailean demanded loudly, his gentle face suddenly a strange mixture of fear and anger. "Did you speak of our time, or bring anyone from the future back to the island with you?" When he saw how his companions were looking at him he said, "'Tis strictly forbidden for druid kind to dwell in any forward time. We may visit, briefly, but only with the approval of the conclave."

"Yet you had no problem with me and the other ladies of the future coming back in time," Kinley said. "Sounds like a double standard to me."

"I dinnae make the rules, my lady," the druid said quickly. "'Tis to prevent druid kind from taking unfair advantage of all the marvels in the future."

His prattle infuriated Catriona. "Unfair, you say? The grove took me to that future after the undead slaughtered every other living soul on Everbay. If no' for the kind mortals who found me, and took me in, I would be dead. I was but seven years old, with no help or training. Gods above, until this moment how could I have ken 'twas even forbidden?"

"Forgive me," Cailean said quickly. "Never has there been such circumstances. Children of the tribes are never abandoned alone as you were."

"My mother and father didnae leave me

by their choice. My uncle had them murdered." Sniping at him wouldn't change any of that, so she said, "Gavin and I willnae use the portal again. We have decided to remain in this time on the island. So naught will be amiss. Now what of this boy the laird mentioned? Why would he be here on Everbay?"

"'Tis a longer story," Lachlan said before the druid could answer her. "One we may discuss at length once we seek a safer place and secure the island."

"You think I'm still enthralled," Gavin said suddenly. "That's why you're tiptoeing around any mention of the undead. I'm no'. The moment Thora took possession of Fenella, my enslavement ended."

Kinley nodded. "Then why did you fake your death?"

"'Tis a longer story, my lady." He eyed the laird. "Thora convinced me that all Pritani were murderous scum. I suppose to her, they were. But I heard the full story during the battle on the skerry, so I ken that your clan isnae what she thought. I would never have left my sister with your men and that Viking if I hadn't."

Catriona knew how much it cost Gavin to admit he'd been wrong—and to say the name he had kept from her. He had said he'd been enslaved by the undead, but not that his master had been his lover. It galled her to think of what he'd been through—and now she understood the pain that had brought him to her isle. Catriona also understood the rush of dark clouds coming from the east. The encounter would not go better in the pouring rain.

"Laird McDonnel," she said, "the storms here can be drenching, and one quickly approaches. Mayhap we should go to my village. You'll be safe there, and we can talk sensibly."

"I personally would love a cup of island brew," Kinley put in.

Lachlan's mouth hitched, and he nodded. The young druid did the same, although he didn't look happy about it.

Holding onto Gavin's hand, Catriona led them through the passage in the cliffs and along the forest trail.

"'Twas a thing I wished to tell you," he said quietly to her. "Why I came to this place."

"It doesnae matter," she said, tucking herself against his side. "And now I ken that it never did. All that matters 'tis that you're here."

While the men remained silent, Kinley proved quite congenial and admired everything she saw.

"What a gorgeous place this is," she told Catriona once they emerged into the glen. "That waterfall was amazing. No wonder you wanted to build a place here, Gavin. It's like your own personal Garden of Eden. Minus the horrible backstory, of course." She grimaced at Catriona. "Sorry. I get chatty when I'm nervous."

"I never expected to meet an American here," she confessed. "What brought you back to our time, my lady?"

Kinley told her own harrowing tale of crossing over as a soldier grievously wounded in action, and how she had landed whole and healed in the midst of a battle between the clan and the undead. As soon as she mentioned her military service Gavin mentioned his own, and they talked of Afghanistan and their time there.

"I don't miss it, for obvious reasons," the laird's wife said. "But it must have been tough for you to take the medical discharge."

"'Twas a blow to my pride," Gavin said. "I'd planned a career in The Black Watch. But Jema kept my spirits up, and looked after me as the ALS progressed." He hesitated before he asked, "How is she, really?"

"She's happy, and busy. She and Tormod are excavating a site in the highlands that dates back a couple of millennia. It might belong to the very first Pritani tribe." Kinley eyed him. "She talks about you all the time with the others. When she finds out you're still alive, she's going to kick your ass."

"The others, my lady?" Catriona asked, trying to keep up with all that she was hearing.

"I'm not the only American time-jumper," the laird's wife said. "We're averaging one new arrival every year. Diana, the detective who was looking for me after I went missing in the future, fell into the same portal that brought me here. Then there's Rachel, an heiress whose husband tried to bump her off to get at her money. She was buried alive in an oak grove. Took us a while to find her."

"You were the first, then," Gavin said, and when Kinley nodded his expression grew thoughtful. "None of you intended to cross over. Like Jema and me, 'twas all accidental."

The laird's wife glanced at Cailean. "That's what it looks like."

Catriona stopped at the barrier, and said to the laird, "Since you are no' druid kind, my lord, you must hold your lady's hand to pass through the boundary." She turned to Cailean, who looked so woeful she almost felt sorry for him.

On the other side of the barrier the laird, his lady and the druid stopped as they saw the village it had concealed.

"I have been coming back a long time now, since the first year after I crossed over to the future," Catriona confessed. She smiled as the animals began to emerge from the cottages to peer at the strangers. "I ken it seems strange, but the undead had torn apart the place. I couldnae forget what they did, no matter how many flowers I planted, so I pleased myself and my animal friends."

Gavin put his arm around her shoulders. "It's beautiful, Cat."

The young druid said nothing, as if he hadn't heard her at all.

"Cailean put in place the spell barrier around your village in his last life," Kinley said in a low voice. "Seeing it now is likely bringing back bad memories." She smiled as a pair of the leverets came bouncing over to her. "Aw, baby rabbits. How adorable."

Catriona could see now the face of the old druid in that of the younger. He kept darting looks at her, too, and twisting his hands in a nervous manner. "Come inside, my lady, and I'll make up that brew. Gavin?"

"We'll follow in a moment," her lover told her.

Inside the cottage she led Kinley to her hearth, where she started a fire and then went to fetch water from the kitchen urn for the brew pot. She had blended several types of herbs and flowers for her brews, and selected a sack with sorrel, red clover blossoms, nettles and dried, slightly-overripe cloudberries for sweetness. To that she added a bit of chamomile, which would help ease tensions.

It surprised her that she didn't feel more nervous. Gavin had been the only visitor she'd ever welcomed to Everbay, and now she was making brew for three strangers as if nothing were amiss. But she sensed the laird and his wife had spoken the truth, and she already liked Kinley, whose frankness reminded her of Senga. Even if the druid was not to be trusted, he had attended to her tribe. If nothing else, she could be courteous to him.

Catriona made up her brew pot with the blend and carried it and every mug she possessed out on a tray to the table by the hearth. There she saw Kinley with a lap full of leverets. "You've made new friends."

"They kept jumping on me until I picked them up. I am never going to be able to eat Meg's rabbit stew again." She stroked one small head as she watched Catriona fill the hearth pot. "The boys will probably stay outside to bicker until the downpour starts, so I hope you put something calming in the brew."

Catriona nodded. "Chamomile." She busied herself with adding wood to build up the fire. "I took him back with me today to meet my family. His disease returned as soon as we arrived, and he fell very sick." She met Kinley's gaze. "He cannae live in his own time again."

"Neither can I." The other woman described the massive injuries and disfigurement she'd suffered during her service, and how she'd been dying just before she'd fallen into the portal. "I was trying to wheel myself over a cliff when I dropped into your time. I had nothing left, and I wasn't interested in a slow, painful death. After I came here I was completely healthy, but then I had to go back to my time. When I came out of the portal I reverted back to the injured and dying soldier I'd been."

"So you and Gavin are the same." It made Catriona's stomach tighten.

"Yes. There's more, too. Jema told me Gavin mentioned committing suicide just before they fell through the dig." Kinley scratched one of the baby hares behind its small ears. "Jema wasn't sick, but since her twin brother was, she had a very good chance at also developing ALS. It's also always fatal. Diana happened to be dying of a brain tumor when she came here, and Rachel had been stabbed in the back, paralyzed, and was bleeding to death. You mentioned something about how you would have died if those people hadn't found you in the future."

"I'd nearly starved while I hid from Uncle, and waited for my mother," Catriona admitted.

The mother hare came in and looked up expectantly at Kinley, who gently began placing the leverets one by one on the floor. "We all have druid blood, we were all facing death, and coming here saved our lives. In your case, same thing, just with you going to the future. What am I missing."

Now she understood. "None of us chose to cross over the first time. 'Twas the sacred oaks that took us. But why? Surely no' simply because we are druid kind."

"I think if that were the case, there'd be a lot more of us." Kinley frowned at the window. "That's odd. It's getting dark already."

"The storm is blocking out the sun." Catriona filled the brew pot to let it steep as she went to look out at the men. Gavin and the laird had walked to the edge of the village nearest the shore, while the druid stood watching the sky and murmuring something to himself. The sunlight had all but disappeared, but she recalled the rainbow that had stretched over Gavin's cottage, and how deeply it had moved her.

A circle soon would close, but how?

Kinley joined her. "Don't mind Cailean. He's pretty upset. The boy who was stolen is his son."

And he the druid who had cast the barrier around the village. He, too, was part of the circle, Catriona thought. "Was it Uncle who took the lad?"

"We're not sure, but Daimh may be involved." Kinley frowned as the laird and Gavin trotted back and with Cailean hurried for the cottage. "Oh, crap. I think we've got new problems."

The men entered just as the rain began to fall. Catriona saw the grim expressions of her lover and the laird, and the druid's blanched face, and knew they were in great danger even before Lachlan spoke.

"We spotted four black ships sailing in fast

from the west," he said. "They'll reach the island within the hour. We cannae fight so many Romans without the clan. Catriona, you and Kinley will come with me back to Dun Aran, where you'll be safe. Cailean and Gavin will wait here in the village until I bring back my men."

She shook her head. "I willnae leave Gavin."

"And I'm sure as hell not going to run back to the castle," the laird's wife said, sounding just as firm. "You can use the spring in the glen to go get the guys. It's closer than the grove. I'll hold the fort here." She waited and watched him. "You know it makes sense."

From the grim expression he wore, Catriona suspected the laird did indeed ken it.

Lachlan seized Kinley, kissed her ruthlessly, and then touched his brow to hers. "Stay alive, Wife." He gave Gavin a long look before he dashed out into the rain.

"If Daimh is with them, then the barrier willnae hold them off," Catriona said. "I've no weapons I can offer you, and they will be too many for three to stand against them. There is a cave beneath the waterfall where I hid when they last came, and they never found me." She gasped as Kinley's hands suddenly burst into flames. "*My lady.*"

"Forgot to mention, I have a built-in weapon." She shook out the flames, and her pale, slim hands appeared unmarked. "I can hold them back for a bit. They catch fire and burn pretty easily, but we need a better defensive position."

"The cliffs," Gavin said. "They'll no' be able to come in from behind us, and if we're overrun we can go through the tunnel and use the grove to escape."

"We cannae leave without Danyel," Cailean said suddenly.

"Lachlan and the clan will do their best to save your son," Kinley said, and then jumped as the cottage door burst open and her soaking-wet husband came inside. "That was quick, even for you, sweetheart."

"I couldnae use the spring to leave. The water within has turned to black stone." He regarded the druid. "'Tis your doing, lad? For we'll no' survive this without the clan."

"No, my lord, I swear to you." He swayed on his feet as if he were about to collapse, and clutched at Gavin's arm. "The McDonnels are the hope to save my son. And if Danyel is killed, then your lady and Diana–" As if horrified at what came out of him, Cailean pressed a shaking hand to his mouth.

"If they'd wanted your son dead, they'd have killed him in his crib," Gavin said to the druid. "Why would they bring him all this way to the island?"

"I don't know," Kinley said flatly. "But in a couple of hours the sun is going to set. Then we'll be up to our ears in undead. So, let's figure this out. How do we get the clan here before the Romans come for us? What do we do to get Danyel away from them?"

Outside the cottage the rain stopped, and all of the sunlight abruptly vanished, plunging the entire island into complete darkness.

"Freyja's Eye," Gavin said, snarling the words.

"No, lad," the laird said. "The goddess herself took back that cursed gem."

Catriona felt as if her bones had turned to ice, but she forced herself to walk outside, and look up at the sky. An enormous, seething black disc hung where the sun should have been, and as she stared at it Gavin came to join her.

"We dinnae have until sunset," she told him in a strained whisper, and pressed her hand against her midriff. "'Twillnae be one. 'Tis Uncle. He's done this."

Chapter Twenty-Two

W HEN QUINTUS SENECA
sailed off to collect the
McDonnel laird, Bryn had
remained on the cliffs until the black ship
disappeared from view. Although she'd
suspected they could no longer see her, she'd
continued to wave her kerchief in the air like a
hopeful lover. Quintus had taken all of his
fellow Romans with him, leaving behind the
newly-turned and woefully-trained. Since no
one of real value to him remained, he'd given
her complete authority over the stronghold.

All this, thanks to Titus Strabo's recom-
mendation, bless his blackened heart.

For the rest of that night she made her
preparations in her chambers, and had her

ladies spread their favors liberally among the garrison to keep the soldiers that remained busy and out of her way. As she worked she dreamed of what she might do once she'd accomplished her purpose. She could take her ladies back to the mainland on one of the black ships, and set up a new, all-female lair in some town with deep cellars and rich men. She might enthrall a noble, have him marry her—in a midnight ceremony, of course—and live as a grand lady by night, holding gatherings and balls so she could have her pick of the local mortals on which to feed.

The possibilities tantalized her, but only one truly satisfied: becoming the first female tribune of the Ninth Legion, with an army of undead females to command, and holding pens filled with enslaved male mortals they could use like whores.

It amused her to think of such fancies, for she would dearly love to see the bastarts who had been abusing females all their miserable lives being forced to perform as they were, with all the humiliation it entailed. She could not guess how many nights the black ship would be away, however, and she could not let this one chance at revenge slip through her fingers before it returned.

The madness that burbled inside her like a black fountain would surely settle then.

The following night Bryn went to the kitchens. The cooks had already returned to their quarters for the night, so the large hall stood empty. Through it she walked until she entered the store room, where the meat, grains and fruits used to feed the island's mortals were kept. There she moved aside a sack of dried apples in the corner to reveal a niche in the wall, from which she took the bottle she had labelled as whiskey and filled the night before with her special brew.

Bryn uncorked the bottle but took care to keep it well away from her nose. The infusion she'd made of wolfsbane root and other, very lethal herbs could do as much damage when breathed in as it would when eaten or drunk. Seeing the colorless tincture made her smile fondly. It always brought back a memory of her father's shop in the village. As a bairn she had sat and watched him carefully preparing his potions and poultices for the local laird and his household. The wealthy paid dearly for their treatments, her da had told her, when all they needed was to cease their excesses.

A pity the facking Romans had never learned that.

Bryn held the tincture at arm's length to tip it over a plate of chopped vegetables and smoked meat, and sprinkled them well. She then returned the bottle to its hiding spot, covered the plate with a thick cloth, and carried it to her private chamber.

There her bed slave greeted her with his whines of love and need, his naked cock rising and stiffening with equal fervor. "Mistress, I didnae think you would return so soon. How may I serve?"

Pathetic, Bryn thought, just as she had been before being turned. The memories of all that the undead had done to her crowded in her head, gnawing at her like a horde of rats.

"You'll eat before you attend to me, for you need to build up your strength," Bryn said as she handed him the plate, and uncovered the food. "Be quick about it, lad."

The mortal began stuffing his mouth, chewing and swallowing so quickly he nearly choked several times. Once the plate had been emptied he grinned hopefully at her. "Now may I pleasure you, Mistress?"

A polite knock sounded on her door, and she smiled. "No' just yet."

Outside stood two of her ladies and one of the newly-turned guards, who appeared to be one of the Hispanians taken as a slave and turned during Ermindale's tenure. Bryn often wondered why the marquess had not survived longer. He must have been as dense as every other undead with a cock.

"Is this the soldier you wished to reward, Mistress?" the younger whore asked.

Bryn nodded, and opened the door wider to admit them. To the guard she said, "My ladies tell me you are the finest lover among the legion." A terrible lie. All the whores feared the Hispanian's brutality. "We give special attention to such men." She gestured to the bed slave. "You may feed on my thrall tonight."

The guard scowled. "Feeding is not permitted while we are on duty, by order of Titus Strabo."

Bryn minced up to him, kissed his cheek, and murmured, "We willnae tell anyone." She stroked the side of his face. "And you look so hungry." She nodded toward her bed slave, who was not yet showing the effects of the tainted food he'd gobbled up. "I've no' yet fed on him tonight. He's just eaten, so his blood will be rich and hot."

That was all it took to persuade the guard. He bared his fangs, and then with three strides seized the bed slave. He bit deep, drinking the mortal's blood as it spurted from the wound. Like most of the newly-turned the guard had not yet learned to control himself while feeding, so even if he tasted any taint in the blood, he would not be able to stop drinking.

Bryn closed the door and locked it, leaning against it to watch as the guard stiffened and released the bed slave, who collapsed.

"Something is wrong." He tottered toward Bryn, almost reaching her before he fell to his knees. "What have you done to me?"

"I've rewarded you," she reminded him. "This was for beating Bridget so badly it took the blood of three mortals to heal her. For tearing into Agnus so savagely that she yet cannae walk without limping. And Gennie here, shall we remind him of what he did to you, lass?"

"He remembers, Mistress," the younger whore said tonelessly.

Bryn waited until he fell forward onto his face, and then walked over to daintily lift her skirts and use her slipper to nudge him onto his back.

"He doesnae turn to ash," one of her ladies muttered. "Mistress, you said 'twould end him."

"The tincture willnae kill him." Bryn bent down and prodded the guard, who remained stiff and staring at nothing at all. "As I thought, it has merely frozen him. Now we must wait and see how long it lasts." She took out the small, sharp blade that she kept tucked in her bodice, and offered it to Gennie. "And what he can feel while it does."

Chapter Twenty-Three

W HILE GAVIN HELPED Catriona barricade her cottage against attack, Cailean went with the laird to cast a spell to reinforce the barrier. Kinley gathered all the old rags she could find, and soaked them with whiskey before stuffing them into empty baskets and crocks.

"Undead bombs. I light them, you throw them," she explained to Gavin as she arranged them on the kitchen table. "Boom." She turned around, inspecting the room. "All I need is something for fuses. Catriona, do you have any wicks or reeds?"

"The angelica stems I gathered might

work if they were no' soaking wet." She looked unhappy as she took down a small box and opened the lid. "Would these do?"

Kinley frowned at the tiny scrolls. "Are these messages?"

She nodded. "I send them to Ennis and Senga by dove, through the portal."

The laird's wife gaped at her. "You can send animals into the future?"

"I must reach into the portal while I hold them, to make it open, and then think of my family, but aye." She stared down at the scrolls and then at Kinley as she realized what the laird's wife had in mind. "It's so dark now. What if Uncle has done something to the portal, as he's done with the spring?"

"I happen to have excellent night vision," the laird's wife said. "As for Daimh, he might know some tricks, but the sacred groves can move people through time. I'll put my money on them."

"Is there a portal near your clan's stronghold?" Gavin asked her.

"Oh, yeah. Right next to it." She grinned, and then frowned again. "Catriona doesn't know where Dun Aran is."

"You do," Gavin pointed out. "You must be the one to release the dove into the portal, my lady."

"And I'd have to get to the portal here before the undead arrive, which with the total eclipse going will be any minute." Kinley bit her lower lip as she thought about it. "I don't have to worry about disappearing. If I do this, Lachlan is going to kill me. But I'm druid kind, so I might reincarnate." She nodded at Catriona. "I need a blank scroll, something to write with, a friendly dove, and the darkest cloak you've got."

Once Kinley had written the message for the clan, Catriona gently attached it to the leg of the dove she brought in.

"Give me a moment, please," she said to the laird's wife, and then held the bird as she looked into its eyes for a long moment. The dove rubbed its head against her chin before it flew to Kinley, and tucked itself inside her bodice, where it nestled with a contented coo.

Gavin knew she might be their only chance to survive, and still hated the thought of sending her out alone. "I should go with you."

"I have fire on demand, and you don't, so you should stay here and be The Black Watch, Captain. Cat, you really know how to train your birds." Kinley wrapped herself in the dark brown cloak Gavin had brought from Catriona's trunk. "All right, I'm heading out. Cat, light some candles so you have them for the bombs if you need them before I get back. Also, don't die while I'm gone. I'll need you two to talk down my husband when he goes nuts about this. See you soon."

Gavin watched her go from the window, and then looked back at his lover, who sat holding her head. "She'll make it to the portal."

"If Uncle hasnae blocked it off, like the spring, aye." She raised her woeful face. "'Tis my fault you'll die tonight. If I'd kept you in the future, you'd have lived a little longer. Mayhap they'd have found a cure, even."

"I'd rather die tonight than spend one more second being eaten alive by that facking disease." He saw her shoulders shake, and picked her up from the chair. Carrying her over to the hearth, he sat down by the fire with her on his lap. "I want to die here, with you in my arms. If 'tis now, then so be it. I'm planning on it when we're both very old and gray and ready for the world after this. Where we go, we go together now, my love."

"I cannae even promise you we shall reincarnate and find each other again." She sighed. "My tribe never returned."

"We couldnae be together in the future," he reminded her as he tipped up her chin. "Then we found each other here." He brushed his mouth over hers, and tasted the salt of her tears on her lips. "'Tis no' an accident, or coincidence. I love you, Catriona, and now I ken that I will forever, in this life and beyond it, wherever we go. Nothing again will keep the two of us apart."

"Three." She took his hand and moved it to her flat belly. "I felt it the morning of the rainbow. The new life we made together grows inside me."

"You're pregnant?" Gavin felt as if she'd clubbed him over the head. "But so soon. How can you be sure?"

"My mother told me that a druidess feels the glow of life the moment we conceive a child," she admitted. "I didnae ken what she meant until I felt our lad quicken inside me last night." She caressed his hand. "If we live, he shall be the first of our bloodline. You can feel him, too, when you touch me."

Gavin focused on her belly, and felt something warm his palm. He stared at her. "Our son did that?" When she nodded he almost laughed out loud, and then understood why she felt so wretched. His own stomach suddenly dropped as he remembered their situation. "I have to get you out of here. You can use the portal to go to Ennis and Senga. They'll keep you and the baby safe."

"I willnae run away from Uncle or the undead again." She climbed off his lap and planted her hands on her hips. "I want my life with you, Gavin. Here, where we belong, with our son. Mayhap with other druid kind we might meet. We can build a new tribe, but first we must fight for it."

A trilling sound came from the window, and Gavin saw Jester flutter down to perch there. The nestling's all-black feathers now showed new white patches, and gray patches on his dark bill. His dull gray webbed feet had grown huge, while the triangle of skin around his bright eyes had taken on a touch of blue.

That was when he stood and saw what none of them had noticed. All around the cottage creatures sat patiently watching Catriona from the little nooks and niches they occupied. The hares and their leverets made a bumpy brown pile in the big basket by the hearth. The eiders had brought several friends. They sat with the female and the nest she'd made beside Cat's kindling box. Two voles sat grooming a third under the table as their tiny young scampered about picking up stray grains from the floor. If she'd had a bathtub, Gavin probably would have seen the shark's fin sticking up out of it.

"You're wrong, love." He stretched out his hand, and Jester flew in to perch on his forearm. "You've already a tribe built."

"I reckon I do." She came to caress the baby puffin's scarred head. "I found his mother on the cliffs when I released him. She knew him by his scent. She'd waited for him, but now he's come back." She took in a quick breath as she looked around them and finally saw what he had. "They didnae scatter when

the Romans came, but they fear the undead,
Gavin."

"Their love for you is stronger." A plan
began to come together in his head. "'Tis the
answer to everything." He transferred Jester to
an armchair, and went to the hearth to pluck a
sliver of charcoal from the embers' edge.
"Would you bring me a gathering sack?"

Catriona fetched the cloth bag, which
Gavin cut apart at the seams and spread out
on the table. He drew on it with the charcoal a
rough outline of the island, and made an x
over the position of the village. Then he
handed her the sliver.

"Draw the barrier and the spring, please,"
he said.

Catriona looked puzzled, but quickly
added a curving line around the village and a
smaller, irregular circle outside it for the
spring.

That gave him enough familiar markers to
add a rectangle for his cottage, wavy lines for
the waterfall, and a circle for the grove portal.

"They willnae leave Danyel on the ship.
They stole him as leverage to use against the
druid and the laird. Where did Daimh breach

the barrier the first time?" When she pointed to a spot close to the spring he nodded. "He wanted everyone in your village to see the undead marching in. He'll likely do the same when they bring the boy to show him. Their full attention will be on Lachlan and Cailean, in fact. They'll no' even notice the animals."

Her shoulders stiffened. "I'll no' send my friends to attack the undead. They'll be torn apart."

"No' to attack," he told her. "To deliver some gifts. Lachlan and I can hold them off from there, to give you time." He explained the rest of his scheme.

Catriona shook her head. "It cannae be me. It must be you." When he started to protest she pressed her fingertips against his mouth. "A warrior doesnae only fight, Gavin. He protects. Just as the Pritani protect the innocent from the undead. I cannae do that as well as you. I think none of us can."

At that moment Lachlan and Cailean came into the cottage, and Gavin knew from the look on the laird's face that their time had run out.

"The undead have come ashore and now

surround the barrier," Lachlan said. "Ovate Lusk has done his best to strengthen the spell wall, but they have Daimh Haral with them. 'Twill only be a matter of time before they break through." He glanced around the cottage. "Where is Kinley?"

Chapter Twenty-Four

✤✤✤

THROUGH THE SHIMMER of the barrier, Kinley saw hundreds of undead marching up from the shore, spurring her into a fast dash for the woods. As long as she stayed inside the barrier, she felt sure she'd remain invisible to the legion, but she was running out of glen. As soon as she reached the rounded corner by the forest, she had no choice but to head for the trail to the cliffs.

"Where is Evander when I need him," she muttered, and then ducked her head and stepped through to the other side of the barrier.

Keeping her pale hair covered with the dark cloak, Kinley darted behind a wide-trunked tree and stopped to listen. The Romans' boots made soft crunching sounds as they pounded their way over the long grasses. The torches the men in the front ranks carried left trails of oily smoke in the air. God, but she hated the heartless, murderous bastards for snatching Danyel. The legion liked to hurt the helpless. She wanted to burn them all, right to the ground, but she couldn't risk lighting up her hands. She might hurt the boy, and the flames she could throw would also give away her position.

The dove in her bodice shifted, but thankfully didn't make any sound.

"Behave, birdie," she said in a bare whisper, and stroked the head that popped up to look at her. "You've got to go save our lives."

Finally, the marching sounds stopped, and she peeked around the tree to see the undead standing in attack formations at the very edge of the barrier. In their center stood Quintus Seneca, dressed in battle armor and his fancy red cape. Another Roman in a dark hooded cloak also stood examining the barrier. Between them a short druid in a shiny gray robe was holding out his hands parallel to the barrier. Black and red sparks flew from his fingers but bounced off the spell boundary to fall and sizzle at his feet.

"Come now, Ovate Lusk," the druid called out in a loud voice. "You ken you are trapped with no hope of escape."

The men kept their eyes on their tribune, and their centurions had stepped forward to create some sort of front line. This was her moment.

Kinley went from one tree to the next, taking advantage of the cover the forest provided until she was out of the legion's sight.

Making her way to the cliffs meant finding her way through the woods in the dark, but once she got away from the legion's torch-bearers her eyesight sharpened and adjusted to the shadows. A few minutes later she reached the entry through the cliffs, and hurried through it into the passage.

"Whew." She stopped for a moment to gently pull the dove out of her cleavage, and cradled it between her hands. "We made it. Now just don't pull me in after you, okay? I'm pretty sure I'd go back to the future and you wouldn't like me so much on the other side. I have Frankenface there."

She didn't hurry as she walked out into the clearing around the portal. Being one slip and fall away from the horrors she'd revisit in the twenty-first century made her extra cautious. The dove grew restless as she stopped outside the carved stones, and turned its head to glare at her.

"Remember, go straight to the castle, and find Evander, or Raen, or just any big guy there." She knelt down, feeling sweat inching down her temple as she reached out and held the dove over the portal.

The carvings on the stone glowed with gold and blue light, and the ground swirled open to reveal a whirling tunnel beneath the surface.

Kinley bent over as far as she dared, and released the dove, who flew down into the portal and disappeared. As soon as it did she snatched her hands away and watched as the ground solidified again. The stone carvings pulsated as she stood and backed up, and she scowled.

"Stop trying to tempt me. Lachlan needs

his personal flame-thrower on this trip." She looked up at the sky, where the sun remained blotted out by the roiling disc of magic. "Just do what you can to keep me from disappearing, okay?"

Going back the way she came worked fine, at least until she reached the glen. More Romans had arrived to add their numbers to those surrounding the barrier, which was now completely cut off. She backtracked and tried to find a break in the ranks, but the Romans had formed an undead barrier of their own.

Kinley stopped under a pine tree, and noticed a branch that had snapped off that still had its needles attached. She picked it up and studied it before she eyed the legion again.

"If you're not going to make a hole," she muttered as she summoned her gift of fire, "then I will."

Setting fire to the branch, she stepped out to fling it at the nearest undead. It landed on the heads of two, who shouted and ran, fanning the flames racing over their bodies and driving away every other soldier around them.

Kinley rushed for the gap they created,

dodging a few clawing hands as she clutched the cloak around her. She had almost reached the barrier when an arm whipped out and clotheslined her, knocking her on her ass.

The big, pale-skinned undead looming over her displayed his fangs, and bent down to grab her. "A female, good."

"Not really good," she said as she drove her boot into his groin, and then rolled onto her feet. "More like great." With more Romans rushing at her from all sides she had to take a running leap to make it through the barrier. "Maybe amazing."

On the other side Kinley fell flat on her face, and got a mouthful of dirt for her trouble. She spat it out as she hoisted herself up and glanced back to see that no one had hitched a ride.

"I should do this rescue thing professionally," she said, feeling rather proud of herself. "Oh, wait, I did." She did a little victory dance, until she saw the man standing and watching her. He had his unhappy face on.

Kinley gave her husband a little wave. "Heya."

Lachlan folded his big arms.

Since he also had that look in his eyes, her least favorite look, she decided to talk very fast. "I got the message bird through the portal. It looked pretty smart, so it'll probably find Dun Aran. I figure, the minute they get it, they'll grab their swords and hightail it over here."

His boot tapped the ground.

"I also warned them about the spring being blocked and all those black ships out there." She waited, and when he didn't say anything she added, "Come on, don't be mad. Someone had to go. Okay, they made me do it."

"No, they didnae." He surveyed her thoroughly. "There are a thousand facking Romans out there, Wife."

"More like nine hundred and ninety-eight," she corrected. "Two are charcoal. Okay, maybe three. It was hard to count while I was fleeing for my life." She batted her eyelashes at him. "And look, I'm alive. I made it. Yay."

Lachlan pointed to the ground directly in front of him, and she trudged over to stand there.

"Can I just say one more thing?" she asked

meekly.

"No. You're the most reckless, mule-headed, thoughtless, irritating wench in all of Scotland," he said sternly. "When we are done with this and return to the stronghold, I am shackling you to the bed. Naked. With guards. Many guards. Mayhap even Evander himself. Then I think I'll have Meg feed you naught but fish and raisin pie for a month. No, two months."

"Boy, you really *are* mad." Kinley wrinkled her nose, and then stepped a little closer. "At any time during my lengthy incarceration, bondage and torture, do I get to play with the snake?"

"Aye." His lips twitched. "But only after I'm done with you." He brushed some dirt from her chin, and then finally dragged her into his arms and held her close. "Fack me, but I love you, you mad wee thing."

Kinley heard a crackling sound, and looked back to see the barrier starting to thin and fill with black and red sparks. "Hold the facking. We're going to need to get some serious defenses up and running. We'd better get back to the village."

Chapter Twenty-Five

S HAFTS OF LIGHT pierced a wide bank of storm clouds to bathe the dark towers of Dun Aran in silver splendor. As Captain of the Guard, Evander Talorc made his rounds of the duty stations three times daily, but also took time in the afternoon to walk with his wife, Rachel, who favored strolling down by the mysterious waters of Loch Sìorraidh.

He simply loved being with her, although his preference would have been privately, in their bed chamber.

"You've been quiet," Evander said. "Have I done something to displease you?"

"Me, no. The men." She shrugged.

"I am Captain of the Guard," he

reminded her. "No' Wet Nurse. Who complained?"

Rachel gave him a mildly exasperated look. "No one ever would."

He grunted. "Who thought about complaining?"

"Sorry, I can't reveal my sources." She bent to pick a bit of heather from the grass. "I will tell you that running defense drills five times a day seems to me…a bit excessive."

"Defending the stronghold, excessive?" He feigned confusion. "I thought it my work."

She eyed him. "And planning to run them five times tomorrow morning before dawn is just plain mean, Evander."

He shrugged. "I've been called worse. I've *done* worse. Talk to Raen, he'll tell you."

"Here's the thing: you have to stop worrying about them," Rachel said, tucking her arm through his. "The laird has gone off more than once to be alone with Kinley. They're probably snuggling together in some secret love nest. Also, you're making the men want to kill you again, and since I like you alive…"

"The men willnae kill me, and the Pritani

dinnae have love nests," he countered, and then saw the look she gave him. "Our cottage in the mountains wasnae that. 'Twas our home while I was a traitorous renegade and you were a poor time-lost lass." He smiled at her. "But I did fall in love with you there, and we did nest, of sorts."

His wife laughed, something that still sent a shiver of delight through his chest. For weeks after she had been buried alive to cross over to him she had barely smiled.

"Thanks for the concession," Rachel said. "Anyway, what I mean is that I don't think you should brood about it until you have reason to worry." Her gaze shifted. "Is that Cailean?"

Evander immediately tensed as he saw the young druid approaching them from the far side of the loch. "No. Rachel, go back to the castle now."

His petite wife didn't move, and when he looked at her he saw her dark brown eyes appeared unfocused, which meant she was using her ability to read minds.

The druid, whose robe looked dusty and stained from a long journey, stopped some yards away and tugged back his hood. He had the face of a young novice, and eyes filled with the knowledge of a man much older. His copper-red hair curled around his unlined features, and he wore a small, carved sea shell around his slender neck.

"Fair day, Captain Talorc, Lady Rachel." The shell swung as he bowed politely.

When Evander glanced at his wife, he saw her pale. She also did not respond when he said her name. Immediately he drew the spear he carried in his shoulder sheath.

"Name yourself and your purpose here," the captain said, "and release my wife from this spell."

"'Tis no' magic," the lad told him, smiling. To Rachel he said, "I am warded against your ability, my lady. You cannae read me, so you mustnae try." Dimples appeared in his cheeks that matched Rachel's. "The ward is some-what mischievous."

She staggered a little before she shook her head, and the color came back into her face. "He's right, I can't read him at all. I got caught in a loop of my own thoughts." She gave Evander a wan smile. "Sorry. I've never encountered a mind like his. It was a little like being trapped in a mirror."

"Whoever you are, you are no' welcome here," Evander told the druid. "Leave now, in peace, or you shall spend the night in our dungeons."

"I cannae go, I fear." The druid looked back over his shoulder. "And neither can they."

Evander blinked a few times, but the hundreds of young druids walking down from the ridges did not disappear. "Dear Gods."

The young druid smiled. "They are, indeed."

Most of the newly-arrived appeared to be the same age as the first. Some wore newer robes and well-made boots, while others sported frayed garments and worn sandals. All of the druid children wore carved pendants made of bone, wood, stone or shell.

"He is like us," one of the young druidesses said, nodding at Evander as she came to hold the hand of the first to arrive. She had hair so fair it appeared silver, and large, beautiful eyes. "So is his lady." She smiled at Rachel. "Dinnae be afraid. We have all seen the grove of stars. We were sent here to you, Captain."

Evander studied the faces behind them, and slowly replaced his spear. "Why would you come to me? Who sent you? The gods?"

The little druidess giggled.

"'Twas Fiona Marphee," the boy druid said. "She showed us how to find you, and said you would help us."

Rachel took hold of his hand, and only then did Evander realize it was trembling. "But Fiona is dead," she said gently.

The boy's face filled with a strange sort of kindness, as if she were the child now. "Aye, my lady." He regarded Evander. "Will you help us, Captain?"

"She bid you to bury her in the sacred grove," the druidess said. "She wished to sleep beneath the oaks. She told you thus when you were alone in the mountains, and she lay dying. No one but you heard her words. Do you remember them still, Captain?"

Evander nearly fell to his knees. "Aye."

"I told you he would," the druidess said.

"So you did." The boy smiled down at her.

"We have journeyed far, and would be grateful for a meal before we leave again."

"Where are you going from here?" Rachel asked.

A messenger dove flew over the boy's head as it headed for the castle's cote. The young druid's expression sobered. "Into darkness, my lady."

Chapter Twenty-Six

CATRIONA FELT ALMOST dizzy with relief when Kinley and Lachlan returned to the cottage. That changed to dismay as the laird described the magic Daimh was using to break through the reinforced barrier.

"'Twill take at least some time for the dove to fly to Dun Aran, my lord," she said. "Will the barrier hold until your men arrive, do you think?"

"From what I have seen, no, lass." The laird exchanged a look with the druid before he said, "We must find some way to stall them. Any suggestions, I gladly welcome."

"Catriona and I can create some chaos," Gavin said, and nodded at the animals gathering outside. "She has the gift to communicate with the creatures who live on the island, and can direct them to help us."

"That explains the very cooperative dove," Kinley said. "What about– *Gavin*?"

Where the highlander had stood there seemed to be only an empty space. Catriona smiled as he came back into sight from the waist up.

"I cannae throw fire, but I can camouflage myself," he told the laird's wife. "When I shift I take on the colors and patterns around me, which renders me virtually invisible. 'Twas how I eluded you all after the battle on the skerry."

"Well, no wonder everyone thought you were dead, Captain Chameleon." Kinley looked slightly disgruntled. "And next time *you're* taking the dove to the portal."

"I can help as well," Cailean said. "I will go to the barrier and speak to Daimh. He willnae see me, but he'll ken my voice. He enjoys prattling, and will wish to boast of what he did to my poor master."

Catriona nodded. "Uncle loves naught better than to puff himself up and preen. 'Tis his pride that troubled my father, for 'twas false. He thought his envy of others led him down the dark path."

Gavin spoke of what they had planned, and Catriona felt glad when the laird agreed with the scheme.

"We'll go to the barrier together," Lachlan said. "'Tis so thin now they may see through it, and we wish them to think us all there, at least until Kinley shows them her fire." He regarded his wife. "We'll need a great ball of it to hurl at them."

She pursed her lips, and then her eyes shifted toward the bombs she had made. "Cat, just how attached are you to that cloak you lent me?"

Kinley and Catriona spread the dark fabric on the table, where they began piling the baskets and crocks of whiskey-soaked rags in the center of it. The men took what was left of her firewood out to the chopping stump behind the cottage.

"We're not sending out these guys, are we?" Kinley asked as she picked up one of the leverets pawing at her skirt.

"They cannae hop fast enough to get out

of the way," Catriona told her, and touched her belly where the little glow of her son warmed her. "Do you and the laird have bairns at home?"

The other woman shook her head. "We can't."

"Ennis and Senga could never have children." She smiled wistfully. "I sometimes wonder if that is why the grove sent me to them, so that we might be to each other what we couldnae have alone."

"Lachlan and I have talked about adopting an orphan, but it would be...difficult." As she finished placing the last bomb on the cloak and gathered up the corners, she didn't elaborate. "But I've been thinking about kids a lot since the undead snatched Danyel from his parents. If the legion ever did that to our kid, I'd go crazy."

"I ken how you feel. I'm with child now." Catriona hadn't meant to blurt it out like that, but she saw sympathy well into the other woman's eyes. "I'm no warrior, my lady. My tribe was killed before I could be trained as a druid. I've lost my parents, my people, and nearly my own life to Uncle. But I willnae allow Daimh to take Gavin or our son from me."

The laird's wife hugged her. "Quit my-ladying me. It's Kinley."

Gavin returned with a small, bulging sack as they were tying up the corners of the cloak.

"I'd best carry that." He handed the sack to Catriona and bent over to kiss her.

"You ken where to go."

She nodded, and embraced him before she stepped back. Gavin always made her feel good inside, but now she felt powerful. "Take care, my great beast."

Lachlan and Cailean waited outside for them, and the five of them walked together to the spell boundary. The barrier had thinned so much it barely glimmered between them and the waiting legion.

Catriona flinched when her Uncle met her gaze and smiled broadly. He gestured to one of the men behind him, who brought a squirming bundle and dropped it at Daimh's feet. A high-pitched yelp came from inside the blanket, and a dark little head poked out to glare up at the druid.

"Fair day, my niece," Daimh said, and

smirked up at the disc blotting out the sun. "Or mayhap no' for you." He gestured to another man who brought a covered basket and set in on the ground. Daimh shifted his eyes to Cailean. "You've done well for an ovate, lad, but your magic cannae match mine. I'll be through this barrier and at your throat before you may blink." He reached down and jerked the boy out of his blanket. "Have you missed your son, Cailean?"

The druid's expression remained impassive, although he did look at the silent child for a long moment.

"I've looked ahead," Daimh said, "and I'm sorry to tell you that wee Danyel here shall be the only brat you ever sire." Daimh patted the boy's head. "The fate of your bloodline rests with him."

Before the laird could reply, Cailean said, "You willnae use my children against me, Haral. Whatever you come here for, you shall no' have it."

"Nor you, Tribune," Lachlan said to the Roman in the red cape.

The other man chuckled. "You've a mortal, a druid, and two women to match against my legion. I rather like my chances this time, McDonnel."

"Do you, Quintus?" Kinley stepped forward, and lit up her hands. "So did Gaius Lucinius. You remember when he and I met? That little pile of ash of him that I left in the clearing? Oh, now I remember. You ran away as soon as the clan showed up. That seems to be your favorite move, running away."

The Roman stepped closer to the barrier to glower at the laird's wife. "I want her as well as the laird," he said to Daimh.

"You can have them all, my lord," the druid said, never taking his eyes from Catriona's face. "I came only for the last Haral."

"Why?" Catriona demanded. "I've done naught to you. I've never exposed what you did that night. I've kept silent all these years."

"True, what you've done, 'tis meaningless to me. But *you*, Niece, *you* are quite everything to me." Her uncle lifted his hands, which turned briefly dark red, as if coated with dried blood. "The Anubis ritual I began twenty years past when I brought the undead is nearly complete. You've only to die, and end our bloodline, and I shall live forever."

Kinley gasped as Lachlan cocked his head back.

"You *facking* bastart," Cailean screamed and lunged at the barrier, and would have gone through it if Lachlan had not grabbed him. "You sacrificed your people to the dark gods for eternal life?"

"Oh, aye. What more could tempt me to leave the faith?" Daimh picked up Danyel, and held the struggling boy like a shield. "You're trapped, outnumbered, and at my mercy, Ovate Lusk. Your son for them. You may keep…" His voice trailed off as he looked past them. "Where is that mortal?"

"Here," Gavin's voice said on the other side of the barrier, and Danyel suddenly jerked out of Daimh's hands. The boy zipped through the air as the highlander shouted, "Now, Cailean."

The druid lifted his hands, murmuring quickly, and the spell wall collapsed. Kinley raised her flaming hands, and threw two fiery plumes at the dark ball that Lachlan hurled at the Romans. The cluster of bombs inside the dark cloak exploded outward, setting fire to dozens of the undead.

In the chaos that ensued, Catriona looked down at the creatures flanking her. She dumped the bulging sack she carried, emptying the slivers of wood wrapped on one end with wet rags onto the ground. Kinley nodded to her, and focused a stream of fire at the slivers, setting them alight.

Be fast, my friends.

Each animal picked up a piece of burning wood from the rag end, and hurried across the barrier. The doves and ducks and puffins swooped down to drop their slivers on the heads of the legion before soaring up into the sky. The hares and voles scampered to place their tiny torches near Roman boots, dodging kicks as they bounded back across to Catriona.

"No," Daimh muttered. His robe flared as he whirled in every direction to see the flaming bodies of the undead fleeing, collapsing, and disintegrating into ash.

The hooded Roman shouted furiously at the men, but the tribune merely stood and stared at Lachlan, who had drawn his sword.

"This shall be the last time you underestimate me, Pritani." Quintus smiled a little before he called out, *"Meus caparum Romanus, impetus."*

Catriona's blood chilled as hundreds more Romans emerged from the shadows and rushed toward the fallen barrier. But in the next moment Gavin thrust Danyel into her arms.

"Run," he told her. "Take Cailean and *run to the cave.*"

⚜

WITHOUT WAITING FOR AN ANSWER, Gavin grabbed Cailean and Catriona's arms, spun them around, and shoved them in the direction of the waterfall. He whirled back to the approaching horde.

"You'll need this," Kinley shouted to him.

He turned in time to catch the tossed blade by its leather-wrapped handle. Though small for his tastes and the grip puny in his big hands, he tested its weight with a wicked slice through the air. He grinned at the laird's wife. It would do.

Fire erupted from Kinley's hands in two blazing streams that tore into the center of the

Roman's front ranks. Though ash plumed into the air and created a wall of gray, more undead ran through it. Kinley let loose with another barrage that lit up the artificial night.

As Lachlan charged left, Gavin attacked to the right. Sword held high, he waded into the pallid creatures as he had once before. Slashing and stabbing, whirling and thrusting, he carved a deep hole into the nearest squad. As they had on the skerry, they turned to ash when they were dealt a killing blow. Gavin didn't waste time on anything else. All he saw were necks, spinal cords, and chests. He plowed through them without a spare movement, sighting his next victim before he'd finished with the current. Soldier after soldier rushed him and though he breathed hard, he realized most could barely use a sword. He parried their haphazard blows as sparks flew from the clashing steel, only to be snuffed out by a new cloud of ash.

But for all their ill-aimed attacks, Gavin's progress slowly came to a halt. What they lacked in skill they made up with something he couldn't battle—numbers.

"To me," Lachlan shouted.

Slowly, Gavin fell back, careful to keep his attackers in front of him. But a quick glance in the direction of Lachlan's voice told him the grim story. The Romans had flanked them. Kinley was burning the undead approaching from behind at a furious rate. Lachlan had his back to her, cleaving two undead in half with every swing of his massive weapon. But as Gavin finally joined them, he could see it wouldn't be enough. There were simply too many.

❀❀❀

CATRIONA LED Cailean past the waterfall and into the hidden cave before handing over his son. In trembling hands, the druid gently clutched the tiny, crying boy to his chest.

"Danyel," Cailean whispered hoarsely, trying to choke back a sob. "Danyel," he said again as his voice failed him and tears began to fall.

Blinking away her own tears, Catriona turned away from them to gather some old linens to dry them all. But as she did, she smoothed her palm down her belly.

My son will be born. I'll no' die today.

When she brought back the old linens to help dry Danyel, she found the little boy had already fallen asleep.

"He's exhausted," Cailean said, his voice shaking, "but otherwise unharmed."

"Cailean," Catriona said gently, "you're about to fall down from exhaustion yourself." She guided him to the small pallet. "Here, lay down with him."

Although Cailean knelt and lay the sleeping boy down, he rose to face Catriona.

"Bhaltair will have me disincarnated for this," the young druid said, "but it cannae be kept secret." He pressed a shaking hand to his mouth and glanced down at his son. "All was nearly lost today."

Catriona placed a hand on his arm. "Your son is safe," she assured him.

"*No*," he blurted out, "no' just my son. He's more than just my son." He moved them both away from the sleeping child and lowered his voice. "I mean…" He swallowed hard. "I mean the Great Design."

"The what?" Catriona said, cocking her head a little. "Do you speak of some druid matter?" She shook her head. "I've no' much training—"

"*No*," he said grasping both her arms. "I mean, yes. 'Tis a druid plan, but only a few know of it. But it cannae remain thus. More must know of it." He glanced at Danyel. "After today, I'm convinced of that."

"Cailean," Catriona said, "now you worry me. Say what you have to say."

"Aye," said a voice from the pallet.

Catriona and Cailean both jumped at the sound. As she pressed a hand over her thumping heart, her mouth dropped open at what she saw.

"Daimh," Cailean muttered.

The old druid hovered over the pallet, dripping wet from the waterfall, and held the tip of a sword over the sleeping child's head.

"Or no'," Daimh said, grinning. "Your prattle doesnae interest me." He fixed his fevered gaze on Catriona. "Only one thing does."

☙❦❧

As the horde closed in, Gavin's mind

flashed to the garden outside his farmhouse, then to the secret village where he'd first met Cat. She would live, along with their unborn child. It was no matter if he died now. It had all been worth it. As he thought of the future that he would not share with her, his heavy arms inflicted a final flurry of parries and blows.

But from the distance came a terrible sound, as though the island had exploded. All heads ducked as an enormous column of gushing water and black stone shot up from the spring. The sky filled with debris as the larger boulders rained down on the Romans who were near it.

"The spring," Kinley gasped. "What the…"

Gavin saw them just as Kinley and Lachlan did. Huge men wearing tartans poured out of the boiling, illuminated waters. Each man held a child, whom they set down on their feet before drawing their swords as the undead turned to face them.

"Clan McDonnel," a tall man with spears in his hands shouted, as he swung down from his back a young boy. "Heid doon, arse up."

He hurled a spear that flew across the glen and impaled two Romans, who burst into clouds of dust.

The clansmen roared as they charged with the spearman at the undead.

Gavin saw the children the clan had brought joining hands in a circle around the spring. Up in the sky the black disc blocking the sun went gray and began to thin.

"Retreat," the tribune shouted from behind the lines as he ran from the glen followed by the hooded prefect. A handful of undead followed them but a mountain of a man with lightning tattoos on his face led a group of highlanders to block the rest. Next to him a man with an axe launched himself into the undead.

"The Viking," Gavin muttered. Then he gazed at the rest of the men. The entire clan must have come.

For once Gavin almost pitied the lifeless creatures who were now in disarray. But the battle was not yet won. The undead still outnumbered the clan. Gavin lifted his sword and advanced with Lachlan and Kinley, just as a bright light washed over the scene.

Shielding his eyes, Gavin saw the disc that had covered the sun was quickly vaporizing. A sparkling beam of multi-colored lights had risen to it from the circle of children. Though Gavin couldn't fathom what they'd done, the effect was clear. Without time to utter but the briefest of shrieks, the legion disappeared all at once. They melted into ashen heaps, their weapons clattering to the ground next to them.

"The tribune escaped, milord," said the mountain man as he came up to Lachlan. "Again. Shall we give chase?"

"Did I call it or what?" Kinley crowed. Though her face was shining with sweat, she grinned madly.

"First," the laird said, eying the children, "I'll ken what manner of help you've brought."

The Viking was making his way across the battlefield, his eyes locked with Gavin's and a smirk crooking his mouth. Gavin found himself smiling in return when a cold realization clenched his chest. Frantically he turned around, his eyes darting across the glen and back again.

"What is it?" Kinley asked, touching his arm.

He turned to her. "Where's Daimh?"

༄༅

"Leave the boy be," Catriona pleaded. "He's naught to you."

As Cailean took a step toward them, Daimh lowered the tip of the sword to the sleeping boy's temple.

"Another twitch from you," Daimh said tightly, "and he dies. And dinnae try any spells, or this 'son who is more than a son' will meet his end now."

Cailean froze. "Do you ken what happens when you dinnae finish a ritual to the dark gods, Daimh?" he asked tonelessly. "They take the promised tribute from you after death—for eternity."

"Oh, they shall have their due very soon," Daimh said. "As shall I."

Still holding the sword so close to the boy's temple that Catriona could barely see a gap between them, Daimh kicked over a rope-bound wicker basket. She and Cailean stared down at it. It was the same one he'd had at the barrier. He must have brought it in. As the lid of the basket rolled away, two red eyes appeared in the inky interior.

"What manner of dark ritual 'tis this?" Cailean demanded.

As if in answer, an enormous snake uncoiled itself and slithered silently forward.

Catriona suppressed a scream as the darkly striated serpent flicked its forked tongue at her.

"Anubis," Daimh intoned to the ceiling as the snake undulated toward her. "Look upon your servant." He grinned at Catriona. "I deliver to you your due, that you may give me mine."

Though bile welled up in her throat, Catriona realized her uncle wasn't going to kill her himself. It would be the same as when he used the undead to kill the rest of her tribe all those years ago. But what Daimh had failed to realize was that her gift was with animals. She stared into the snake's glassy red eyes.

Master snake, she thought to the creature. *I am not your enemy.*

Though she had never tried to converse

with an animal, it seemed to have an effect. The great serpent stopped its approach. A strange rasping sound filled her mind and though she shuddered at its cold touch, she did not cringe away. Not only did her life depend on it, so did that of her unborn child. But words were not going to work. Instead she focused on her memories of the slaughter. Image after image rolled forth from the past, culminating in her hiding in this very cave.

"Anoup!" Daimh said. "Take her!"

In response, the viper lifted its enormous diamond-shaped head and opened its jaws. Though its fangs glistened in the dim light, it stayed where it was. Catriona opened her thoughts to it, and strange distorted images came to her: prey kept just out of its reach, the dark inside of the too-small basket, and Daimh's gloating face.

Him, Catriona thought. She pictured the same gloating face she'd seen when her tribe had been massacred. *Him*.

Slowly, the snake turned its head toward her uncle.

"Anoup!" Daimh screamed, the sword shaking erratically in his hand. "Kill her!"

Cailean leaned forward just as the cascade of water behind Daimh briefly parted.

"Cailean," she whispered. "Don't move."

Suddenly the sword was snatched away as Gavin appeared behind the old druid. With a great shove, he sent Daimh flying—directly at Anoup.

In a blur, the viper shot forward. Before the druid could hit the ground, the snake's fangs sank into his throat. Cailean lunged for the pallet and scooped up the still sleeping Danyel. Gavin swept Catriona into his arms and away from the pair on the ground.

As the four of them looked on, Daimh writhed. Catriona's stomach heaved, and she wanted to turn away, but she forced herself to watch this last horror. This would be the only justice she would ever have for her tribe.

Though her uncle's mouth opened, he could make no sound. Catriona covered her mouth as Daimh slowly succumbed to the venom. As the light left his eyes, the snake released its hold. Gavin snatched up the sword and put himself between the creature and Catriona.

"Wait," Cailean said. "Look." Like its

victim, the viper began to slowly writhe. Cailean pointed at Daimh's neck. A radiant black liquid was oozing from his wounds. "The dark magic." As the jaws of the great snake opened and closed one last time, it finally stopped moving. "Gods have mercy," Cailean whispered.

Danyel chose that moment to rouse, and reached up to pat his sire's face.

"Da."

"Aye, my lad," the druid said, and kissed the top of his head. "'Tis done."

Chapter Twenty-Seven

GAVIN LED THE way back to the edge of the glen, now bathed in sunlight. Gray ash whitened the lush grasses, and a few small fires still smoldered. Broken black rock surrounded the spring, and huge puddles of water swamped the surrounding soil. The clan stood with their laird and lady as they spoke with the copper-haired spearman, and swung around with hands on their sword hilts the moment they spotted Gavin. They relaxed almost immediately, yet still remained in protective ranks around Lachlan and Kinley.

The laird walked out to meet him. "'Twas a glorious victory." His gaze shifted to Cailean. "The boy?"

"Safe and no' a mark on him, my lord," the druid said. "Thanks to you, your men, Gavin and Catriona."

Kinley made a scoffing sound. "Come on, I want credit for doing the most damage. Well, me and the rabbits and puffins and sunshine." She kicked a pile of ash on the ground. "A few got away with your uncle, but not enough to form even a tiny little Roman detachment. The legion is toast."

"Daimh is dead," Catriona told her, and gave a brief account of what had happened in the falls cave, and added, "We cannae thank you enough for saving us, my lady, my lord."

"How did your men come through the spring and Daimh's enchantment?" Gavin asked.

"It was the druid children," the laird answered.

Catriona glanced around them. "Where are they?"

"Our new friends went to have a look around the village," Kinley said. "Come on and we'll introduce you."

Gavin took her hand when she hesitated. "You've always wanted to meet other druids."

"I ken, 'tis just..." She grimaced and touched the front of her skirt. "I've such an odd feeling. 'Tis like the baby dances inside me."

They walked from the glen to the village, now filled with the young druids. Some ran about chasing each other and Catriona's animal friends, while others stood before the cottages holding hands. All of the children turned and smiled as Catriona and Gavin drew closer.

The oldest among them walked up with a younger girl skipping alongside him. "Fair day to you, my lord, my lady." He looked all over Catriona before he said to the girl, "I ken she would be tall with those long legs of hers."

The little druidess shrugged. "'Tis no' always so. I had long legs." A comical expression of disgust filled her face as she glowered down at herself. "I'm even smaller this time."

Gavin felt his lover shaking, and bent his head to hers. "If 'tis too much for you, sweet Cat, my cottage awaits."

She swallowed hard and shook her head. "I'll be well again. 'Tis just I cannae believe it." Still holding his hand, she walked up to the children. "Why come now? Why no' before this?"

"For some years we waited," the older boy said. "You had found your place in the future, and we wished you to be safe as well as happy." His expression darkened. "We thought Daimh might watch for us, too, and use us. We couldnae permit that."

The druidess's small face grew weary. "Aye, so we abided in the well of stars until we thought enough time had passed. Even then we had to be clever. None of us came back in the same year, or to the same tribe. We scattered ourselves across the land, among the smaller, remote settlements." She kissed the boy's cheek. "My brave one came first, to learn how to ward himself and the rest of us. Our families thought us strange, for they couldnae sense our souls, but still loved us."

Catriona drew in a sobbing breath. "Will you go back to them? Your new families?"

"We can if we must," the boy said, and looked around them. "We would rather reveal ourselves, and form a new tribe. We dinnae wish to dwell here, for 'tis a dark place to us."

He smiled at Gavin. "And you and your high-lander dinnae wish to hide any longer, either."

Gavin felt completely perplexed. "Who are you children?"

The boy sighed. "You shall both need much training, my son. We have but the bodies of children. Our souls have reincarnated. I'm called Teren now, and my dearest love is named Isabeau. Before this life, we were Tavish and Isela Haral."

Catriona slipped from Gavin's grasp and fell to her knees before weeping into her hands. But the little druidess came to wrap her small arms around her.

"Oh, dinnae cry, Daughter," Isabeau said, stroking her hair. "I promised you that I'd come for you."

Gavin looked around the village at all the other children. "Does that mean what I think?"

"Uh-huh." Kinley's eyes grew dreamy as she gazed at the young faces. "They're all reincarnated souls of the Moon Wake tribe."

IN THE BOWELS of the black ship, Quintus Seneca felt the last rays of the sun vanish again from the sky. He paced the length of the light-tight compartment, his uniform still shedding ash from the battle. Unable to bear the flutter of his scarlet battle cloak, he tore it from his shoulders and flung it to the deck.

The disastrous battle had destroyed all but a handful of his men. All he had left were the five that had reached the black ship before the sun-disc dissolved, and the useless recruits he'd left behind on Staffa.

The glorious Ninth Legion wasn't simply finished. It no longer existed.

Heavy footsteps trudged down the stairs as Titus Strabo climbed down into the cargo hold. His dark hood and cloak had been covered with so much undead ash they looked pale gray now, and when he revealed his face his eyes glittered with contempt.

"Report," Quintus snapped.

"Report...what, Tribune?" The prefect took the final step to plant his feet on the deck. "We were defeated, resoundingly so. A thousand men, now dust. Three ships left behind, burning along with their undead crews. The turncoat druid, vanished. The McDonnels rally around their laird, happy in their victory. Again." He gestured toward the stairs. "It is safe now for you to come up. The captain wishes a word with you." He started back for the upper decks.

"Strabo, wait," Quintus said quickly, drawing him to a halt. "You were correct in your advice to me, and I not wise enough to accept it. I am sorry. Truly, for you and for the loss of so many, but we cannot allow it to defeat us. We will rebuild the Ninth. We shall have our vengeance."

"Yes, my lord," the prefect said before he left.

Quintus shook out his cloak, replacing it before he dusted off his uniform and cleared his thoughts. What he had to do now was inspire loyalty. He knew of only one manner in which to do that.

Up on deck, the cold night wind rushed over him as he stepped out, making his cloak flutter. He saw Strabo standing with most of the mortal crew at the stern, while far fewer undead occupied the bow. The prefect held a long dagger, which he raised above his head.

"This madness ends now," he shouted, staring past Quintus at the other undead. "We are barely a hundred left, if that. Too many Roman lives have been sacrificed on the altar of Quintus Seneca's idiocy. As a Roman, and the prefect of the Ninth Legion, I condemn him to his fate."

Quintus stood waiting as Strabo strode toward him, his murderous mortals crowding after him. The tribune looked over at the navigator, and gave him a small nod.

The mortal tugged on a rope hanging from the deck, which tipped over the bucket of lamp oil he had secretly rigged there at Quintus's command.

The oil splashed down on Strabo and his mutineers, causing them to slip and fall onto the deck.

"I have defeated more assassination attempts than you might count, Prefect. Serving under Gaius Lucinius taught me that." He felt no joy as the navigator handed him the flaming torch. "You should not have hidden the weapons, you know. I'd have had no idea of your plot if you'd left them out in plain sight. I never have paid attention to the stores of arms. Oh, but you were quite right about the druid. In the end he proved to be traitorous scum."

He tossed the torch on top of the pile of oil-soaked bodies. The mortals screamed and flung themselves over the railings, but Strabo remained crouched on the deck, his uniform flaming and the untouched side of his face blackening as he stared at Quintus. He said nothing, and when the flames ate through his skin he fell to the deck as ash, snuffing them out.

"How noble." Quintus glanced down at the burned mortal crewmen treading frantically in the sea, and gestured for the navigator. "Bring some archers here and finish them."

The mortal bowed. "As you command, Tribune."

He walked to the bow of the ship, where his remaining soldiers averted their gazes. Fire had left black scorch marks on their armor, and the dust of their comrades grayed their faces. He counted three he recognized from their original ranks, but the rest were mortals and slaves they had turned undead.

Counting himself, the Ninth Legion had been reduced to just four Romans.

"I do not blame you for refusing to come to my aid," he told them. "I do thank you for choosing not to help Strabo kill me." He looked at each of their sullen faces. "When we arrive at the stronghold, you shall have your pick of the mortals, or the undead whores being trained, if you prefer. You may do as you wish with them for as long as they live. There will be many to go around now."

The men gave each other uncertain looks.

"It is not a trap," Quintus promised them. "I value each of you. I wish to earn back your trust. This is a new beginning for the Ninth Legion. We will learn from this tragedy. We will be stronger for it. But if you still feel that I do not deserve to live, please, come forward. Share in Titus Strabo's glorious mutiny, and die in flames."

No one moved.

"My thanks." He deliberately turned his back on them. "Dismissed."

Chapter Twenty-Eight

✤✤✤

CATRIONA WOKE UP to the sound of rain pelting the thatched roof, and the soothing rhythm of Gavin's heartbeat thudding under her cheek. Her unborn son lay sleeping inside her, his presence like a tiny candle flame. For a time she simply lay with her eyes closed and relished the sounds and sensations of her life. She had faced Uncle, achieved justice, and found her tribe again. She carried the child of the man she loved. She almost laughed when she realized that because of Gavin, every one of her most precious dreams had come true.

Something made a purring sound, and the little paw inked on her belly stretched just as the big man under her did.

"I ken you're awake," he said, his voice deep and drowsy. "You snore when you're asleep."

She lifted up her head. "What? You lie."

"Like a wee kitten. It drives me mad for you." He brushed the rumpled hair back from her brow, and traced his finger down the length of her nose. "We dinnae have to leave today. The laird can wait."

"Aye, Lachlan McDonnel, awaiting our leisure with his great clan of highlanders looking after my tribe of bairns in their great dark castle hidden from all on an island. Teren will have to show us the way." She kissed his chest. "We should have gone to Dun Aran yesterday."

"Our tribe." Gavin curled his arms around her and shifted her so that the curves of her bare breasts brushed his chin.

When he did that she wanted to put her nipples against his mouth—which was likely his aim. "What did you say?"

"Our tribe. No' your tribe." He nuzzled her there, breathing in the scent of her skin before he rubbed the tip of his nose against the tightening peaks. "Teren agreed to initiate me, once I've learned a bit of Druidry. Evidently being a color-changing warrior only makes me a great lizard."

An urgency spread through her as soon as he moved her up against him to suckle her sensitive breasts. "And then, when you've had your training?"

He growled something and rolled over with her, tucking her under him. "I'll be a druid proper."

"And today you'll be my mate," she said. The feel of him rooting between her thighs made her bones go liquid. "Mayhap we could go after midday."

"Oh, aye," Gavin murmured as he lowered his mouth to hers, and slowly pushed into her.

All the fear and loneliness that had followed her to the island had gone along with her uncle, and now Catriona had Gavin. Being with the man she loved made up for all the long, empty years. When he came into her she could feel the surge of his beast spirit, now much gentler since she had conceived. It moved inside her with Gavin's thick, hard shaft, stroking her and him with pulses of heat and hunger.

"Yes, Cat, sweet lovely soft woman. You feel so good under me. I want to do this to you every morning. I want to bring you over and over, until you never want to be anything but naked and with me."

His words made her gush with wetness around him in response, and he pumped deeper.

"That wouldnae be wise, my beast." She looked up into his eyes as he buried himself deep in her. "We've a baby coming. He'll want more than parents who willnae leave their bed."

His mouth curved as he slid his hand between them to cover their tiny son. "So he will."

Without warning he withdrew from her, making Catriona cry out in frustration, and then make a very different sound as he slid down and put his mouth to her damp quim. Gavin stroked her open with his tongue.

Catriona gripped the bed linens as Gavin suckled her, his mouth so hungry she had to muffle another cry with the pillow. Then he pushed his fingers into her, working them in and out of her clenching opening.

"Gavin," she breathed.

"That's what I want, oh, aye, my beauty, my lady. Let me have all your pleasure now. Drench me with it."

They spent the rest of the morning in bed, making love and talking. They rose only to make a brew and have some fruit and morning bannocks, and then to heat water for bathing. That ended with more love-making, as they couldn't seem to stop touching each other when they were naked. When they finally emerged from the cottage the sun had begun its descent toward the west. Catriona felt glad to see no more dark smoke from the burned black ships tainting the sky. The rain had also washed away much of the signs of battle from the glen. She would always love Everbay, but it no longer felt like her home.

Gavin was that now.

She spotted two figures walking up from the glen, and squinted against the sunlight. One appeared to be a clansman from the McDonnel tartan he wore, but he was fair-haired and carried an axe instead of a sword. The woman beside him had long, gleaming golden hair, and wore trews and a tunic instead of a gown, but even at this distance Catriona could see she wasn't Kinley.

Beside her Gavin went utterly still, and then Catriona knew who the couple were.

"We could leave for Skye now," she said quietly, and took his hand in hers. "If you wish."

He glanced at her. "No, lass, I only thought I wouldnae see her until we went there, if at all." His mouth hitched. "She couldnae wait to confront me. She never can."

They walked down to meet the couple, both of whom wore stern expressions. The clansman definitely had the look of a Viking, Catriona thought, as did the woman. She also saw in miniature Gavin's chin and his brows on Jema Liefson's face.

They stopped a few yards apart, like opponents on a battlefield, Catriona thought. No one said anything at first, and the silence stretched out so thin and tense that she wondered if either of them could speak to the other. Then she understood. This woman was

Gavin's twin sister. She was so angry with him that she didn't trust herself to speak.

"Well?" Tormod Liefson said. "You've no' seen each other for almost a year. You cannae have changed so much. You're twins. Have at it."

"You bastard," Jema said, her voice like ice. "You made me think you were dead. You ran away to hide. One message, that's all I'd have needed."

"Why? You were glad to be rid of me," Gavin said, sounding lofty. "You didnae even bother to check that I drowned. I understand, Jema. I ken what you had to do for me when I was sick. It wore you down."

"Oh, aye, right, you ken. Worn to the bone, I was, loving you and looking after you and trying to keep you alive. And you think I wished you dead so I could be free of you?"

His sister's eyes narrowed as she stretched out her hand to Tormod, who gave her a silken sack. Still looking at him, she pulled out a piece of clothing that he recognized. It was the jacket he'd worn that day they'd fallen through time.

"Where did you—"

"In the little cottage near the burial mound," Jema snapped, shaking it at him. "I was so keen to be rid of you that I sought you out even when you were supposed to be dead." Her eyes began to glisten. "Night after night I dreamt of you." Her lower lip trembled as she bunched the fabric in her fist. "Then yesterday, I thought you truly had…"

"*Jay*," he said, his throat tight. "'Twas bitterness at how Thora had used me. I saw your new life with your Viking and the clan—and it ate at me that you were happy without me."

"*Gee*," she sobbed, "I never stopped thinking of you."

He held out his arms and she rushed into them. "Forgive me, Jay," he said into her hair. "It was a madness."

Gavin felt her nod silently against his shoulder and kept holding her tight, unable to speak past the constriction in his own throat.

"He loved her," Catriona said. "Twelve months gone, and he still mourned her—and you. 'Tis time for the grieving to be over."

Jema separated from him and nodded as

she wiped her eyes. "We've no' been intro-duced," she said to Catriona.

"I am Catriona Haral. You might remember me as Iona Errol in the future."

"The gardener's daughter?" Jema looked from Catriona to Gavin and back again.

"'Tis a long story," he said, bringing Catriona to his side. "But you should know that she carries my son—and your nephew."

"A child?" Jema exclaimed, sobbing anew as she threw her arms around them both.

Tormod took a step back, and caught Catriona's eye. "I'm Viking," he explained gravely. "We dinnae do group hugs."

Chapter Twenty-Nine

Q UINTUS DIRECTED THE captain of the black ship to take a convoluted route back to the Isle of Staffa. He would not risk any of the McDonnels' mortal allies reporting back to the clan about his movements and inviting a direct attack on the lair.

It took four days to return, and by the time they dropped anchor the remaining undead were on half-rations to preserve the last of the living thralls. Quintus himself suffered the new torments of blood hunger, and only just managed to maintain his dignity around the crew.

Strabo's betrayal had injured him much more seriously than he'd first imagined. On the journey back to the lair Quintus often spent hours pondering every aspect of his relationship with the prefect. He had given him rank, respect, and trusted him with responsibility—this after he had been maimed, no less —and he had responded with treachery, lies and hatred.

Perhaps it was the difference between men and women, that males ever envied their betters, while women wished to nurture them. Fenella would never have tried to kill him. Oh, certainly she had threatened to, but he had always known she would not. After all, she had been his creation. She had loved him as a mortal, and protected him with her life as undead. He would never know the like of her again, no matter how long he lived.

Strabo had been the embodiment of all his failures.

A crescent moon hung over Staffa as the black ship dropped anchor, and Quintus gave the order to lower the spare dories so they might depart immediately.

As his men rowed him across the last stretch of sea, Quintus peered ahead, and smirked a little as he saw Bryn Mulligan, dressed like a queen and waiting with her ladies. That a whore could think herself so important to him was as ludicrous as Strabo believing he could assassinate his way to becoming tribune.

Quintus waited until the men had dragged the small boat onto the rocky shore before he disembarked, and walked up to where the undead females waited. "Bryn, how kind of you to come to greet me."

"I've thought of nothing else since you left, Tribune." She dropped into a deep curtsey before she offered him the goblet of blood she held. "You come back much later than I expected. Indeed, I feared you never would. Do we celebrate your victory over the clan?"

"I think you can see such did not happen." He snatched the goblet and greedily drained it in a few gulps. "I am obliged to make some changes now. Things will have to be a little different, but I'm sure you and your ladies are up to the task. All you must do is what I tell you." He met her placid gaze. "There shall be but one rule now: obey me or die."

"'Tis a very good rule," Bryn said warmly. "Might I borrow it?"

He considered her request. Since she looked after the females with no complaint, he should allow her to keep a little authority. "With your ladies, of course."

The other whores brought goblets to his starved men, who drank them down with relish. Quintus gestured for Bryn to walk with him into the stronghold, and as they did he told her that Strabo had betrayed and massacred the legion by conspiring with the druid. As he spoke the hot blood in his belly seemed to grow cold and thicken into ice.

"Strabo is dead," the tribune said, "and the druid vanished, but I yet live. As long as I do, the legion will go on. I *am* the legion." He felt an unfamiliar languor coming over him, and then noticed that no sentries had been posted at the front stations. "Where are the guards?"

"'Tis a surprise. You'll see, just inside." As Quintus stumbled, Bryn took firm hold of his arm. "I cannae wait for you to see what changes *I've* made."

Chapter Thirty

❧❦❧

AS GAVIN AND Catriona approached Dun Aran, it seemed to him that night had turned to day. Tall, staked torches blazed in opalescent colors all along the path to the great castle. Next to the loch two bonfires sent dazzling sparkles flittering into the air. The torches along the battlements were lit, as were those that ringed the entrance. Everywhere there was activity.

Robed druids were putting the finishing touches to a white wedding arbor between the bonfires. Its graceful, interwoven branches stretched skyward, creating an arched dome. Sprays of gay color dotted its latticework frame, and Gavin recognized some of the flowers that Catriona favored, including lavender.

Highlanders were carrying out tables and chairs, followed by women with platters of food. But what made Gavin smile most was not the preparations. It was the children who ran everywhere, their faces beaming.

"They are so happy," Catriona whispered beside him as she gripped his hand tighter. "Even now, I can scarce believe they're here."

Gavin felt as though he were getting a crash course in the ways of the magic folk. "I ken what you mean."

Jema and Tormod came down the path from the castle. In their beautiful, matching tartans, he had never seen his sister look more beautiful. Nor would her beauty or youth ever dim. After swearing fealty to the clan, he and Cat had been told of their immortality. They had been shocked—and yet not, given all they'd witnessed.

Jema's eyes had turned sad. "I'll outlive you, Gee. I don't know if I can stand to see it."

"You were ready when I had ALS," he'd gently reminded her. "But you'll only have to wait 'til I reincarnate. I'll find you, Jay. 'Tis fated."

As two of the young Moon Wake tribe ran laughing across their path, Tormod snorted. "We're hip-deep in bairns." His shrewd blue eyes softened as Isabeau came skipping over to hug Catriona around the waist. "Ah, well, someone has to take charge of them."

"You two are a sight," Jema beamed. She leaned in to give them both a peck on the cheek. "Gavin makes for a dashing groom in tartan, and Catriona, you're lovely in that gown."

"I am forever in debt to you and your seamstress for it."

"Did you bring the cord for the handfasting?" Gavin asked Tormod.

"Aye," the Viking said. He held up a short section of rope but eyed it doubtfully. "'Tis druid custom to take the bride prisoner?"

"'Tis a symbol only," Catriona assured him, "of being bound one to the other."

Gavin saw the laird and his lady sitting with Teren and Cailean, and another, older druid wrapped in a thick wool blanket. "Who is the old man?"

"Master Bhaltair Flen," Jema told him. "The wisest and kindest of the magic folk."

"He's the druid my uncle tried to kill before he left for Everbay," Catriona added in a lower, subdued tone.

"'Twas naught of your doing, Cat," Isabeau scolded in her piping voice. "Master Flen understands this. Now come, sweetheart. I'll introduce you."

Tormod watched the pair go before he said to Gavin, "Hearing a mother's voice come out of that wee little thing should be troubling, but oddly, 'tis no'."

"You've seen me possessed by a Viking goddess with one eye," his wife reminded him. "Everything after that should be cake."

A short, bald man with war hammers tattooed on his arms hailed Tormod and Jema, who excused themselves to go and speak with him. That left Gavin to follow after his wife and her reincarnated mother. Lachlan stood as soon as he saw him and clasped arms with him.

"I'll send for Cailean and the others," the laird said before he made introductions.

Gavin went down on one knee before the

old druid. "Master Flen." He bowed his head. "'Tis an honor."

Despite the obvious signs of his recent brush with death Bhaltair's dark eyes shone brightly as he surveyed Gavin.

"Well, then, lad. You're the hero of Everbay Isle now. You saved your lady, the boy, and my ovate. Then, too, you and your lady kept a madman from attaining eternal life at the expense of so many others. No' what we expected of you a year past."

Gavin nodded. "I'll try to keep surprising you, Master Flen."

"You've both done that." The old man gave Catriona a decidedly fond look, and gazed around them at the happy druid children. "An entire tribe of souls, scattered and then come back like this. 'Tis never happened in any generation. We cannae fathom it. 'Twill be the talk of the conclave for centuries."

Gavin saw the laird smiling, which seemed like a good omen. "What will happen to the children now?"

"They wish to reform their tribe," Bhaltair said. "After what they suffered, we cannae think of a reason to deny them." Bhaltair nodded at Cailean as he arrived. "Nor shall I stand in the way of my ovate choosing his new path."

"I go to live in the household of the Gordon Clan," the younger druid explained. "I'm needed there to help protect the Countess and her son." He nodded to Raen and Diana as they arrived, and also Evander and Rachel. "But such news 'tis not why I awaited your arrival." He and Bhaltair exchanged a long look but the older druid finally nodded.

"You're killing me with the suspense, Grandpa," Diana said.

"What news demands the seneschal, the captain of the guard, and the laird?" Evander asked.

"Your wife has had some glimpse of it," Cailean replied to him but looked at Rachel. "She saw it in my mind."

Bhaltair's eyebrows flew up but Rachel only smiled and looked at the ground.

"Not sharing, are we?" Kinley quipped, but gave Rachel a wink.

Lachlan held up his hand. "Allow the man his say."

There was silence and all eyes turned to Cailean.

"We have long wished mortal kind to share our path," Cailean said quietly. "'Twas decided that we would begin our Great Design…" He glanced around the circle. "By secretly siring children with mortal ladies."

"What say you?" Raen demanded.

Diana patted his massive arm. "Like me and Bhaltair, big guy. It's all in the family."

"Danyel," Catriona whispered.

"Aye," Cailean said. "I nearly told you in the cave." He turned to Kinley. "I thought you would see it when you met Bethany. Your hair and eyes are no' the same, so I didnae recognize it at first, but your face… I see her now every time I look upon you."

The laird's wife caught her breath sharply. "Oh, no."

"Just as Lady Diana is Bhaltair's, so you are mine," Cailean told her. "When my son is grown, he shall sire your bloodline."

"If Danyel had died," Kinley said, "I'd never have been born. Diana would never come looking for me. We'd both disappear."

Cailean nodded but the laird looked skeptical. "What has any of that to do with sharing the druid path?"

"It's a very primitive form of genetic engineering," Jema said before Cailean could reply. "They're trying to change the future."

"Of mortal kind, aye," Cailean said. "We hope by this that someday all will be druid kind, and share our path. The time shall come when all may reincarnate, and learn from their past lives, and find true enlightenment. Death would never again hold dominion over any of us."

A hushed silence followed.

"Giving everyone on the planet a shot at immortality?" Kinley said, her mouth crooking up in a half grin. "That's a pretty ambitious plan, even for the truly enlightened. How will you know if it worked?"

"You are the proof of it, Wife," Lachlan told her. "You are druid kind, and yet you have never been reborn. Nor have Diana, Rachel or Jema."

"I cannae say why you are come back to us," Cailean admitted. "'Twas no' part of the Great Design. The gods havenae revealed their purpose. 'Tis baffling."

"But after the threat to Danyel," Bhaltair said, "'twas clear that the Great Design could no longer be our secret." He looked over his shoulder to the preparations still taking place in the distance. "But 'tis no' a matter to be shared with more than those here." He gave Lachlan an appraising look.

The laird slowly nodded. "Aye. 'Twill no' be spoken of." He looked at each of the highlanders and their ladies, all of whom nodded. Gavin and Catriona both met his gaze and agreed as well.

"So then," Bhaltair said. "With Cailean moving to the Gordon household, we're in need of an official liaison between the conclave and the clan."

Lachlan smiled at Gavin. "I wish to offer the post to you, McShane."

That startled a laugh out of Gavin. "My lord, I'm no' even a druid yet."

"You're druid kind, which counts," Kinley told him. "You'll get lots of on the job training, and we'll need you here to help build the new settlement. We were just discussing it."

Gavin looked at his lady. "I've missed a great bit of this talk, I think."

"The Moon Wake tribe have the souls of men and women," Catriona said, "but they cannae live so until they're grown. They've also still the nature of the young in many ways. They'll need older folk to look after them, and act in the place of parents when need be for the mortal world."

"No one will believe that Cat and I had this many children," Gavin pointed out.

"That's why we want to help," Kinley said. "The clan can't reproduce or adopt mortal orphans. But a tribe of druid kids who know what we are, and would be happy to stay on Skye…perfect match."

"Teren has spent much time together with my lady and me since he came," Lachlan put in. "We'd be glad to help."

"Your mother would not ask her own daughter to raise her," Rachel said. "But the captain and I have been taking her to pick flowers by the loch. She's a good match to our own quiet."

"I…" Catriona began as emotion choked her voice. "I dinnae ken what to say."

"If I may," Gavin said. "I'll ask a moment to speak with my lady."

Gavin offered her his hand, and led her to the arbor.

"We've come full circle, Cat," he said as he stopped beside the fragrant lavender. "That's what you said the morning the rainbow came. You and I began among the flowers like this. Mayhap it was always meant to be."

She nodded, and slipped into his arms.

He held her as he looked out at the loch sparkling in the moonlight. Between them the glow of their unborn child began to expand, as if he wanted to warm them both. Gavin drew back to look all over his lady's lovely face.

"I've always wanted a hundred kids," he said gravely.

"I grew up alone," Catriona said softly. "I wanted three hundred."

"We talked about starting our own tribe," he reminded her. "We'll no' have to do that. And you'll have a chance to boss around your mother for a few years, something I think every daughter secretly desires."

"Then we'll accept. Only ken that I have you, Gavin McShane." Standing on her toes, she kissed him. "'Tis all I'll ever want."

"Aye, my sweet Cat. You are my world. Now come and let us make use of this arbor."

THE END

• • • • •

Another Immortal Highlander awaits you in Brennus (Immortal Highlander, Clan Skaraven Book 1).

For a sneak peek, turn the page.

Sneak Peek

Brennus (Immortal Highlander, Clan Skaraven Book 1)

Excerpt

CHAPTER ONE

Wedged in a corner beside a wooden bin, Lily Stover listened to the winter wind wailing outside the granary. Silly as it seemed, she wished she knew what time and day it was. Her watch had been smashed during her last beating, and calendars probably hadn't yet been invented in fourteenth-century Scotland. She'd tried keeping count in her head, but the rottBeing a redhead in Scotland helped Althea Jarden blend in with the locals, at least until she spoke. Although she'd lost most of her southern accent while working on her Ph.D. at Cornell, whatever she said broadcast her as an American. Fortunately, no one held that against her. The Scots she met were more curious as to why she wasn't out shopping, taking a tour of Fort George, or snapping photos of Loch Ness in hopes of spotting its infamous monster.

"I'm just here for the ferns," she told the innkeeper and his wife as she checked out at their front desk. "I'm a field botanist working for the University of Glasgow. We're researching hart's-tongue fern's chemical components and mechanisms of action." When the couple's jaws sagged she quickly added, "I collect and test plants to make new medicines."

"Och, like my Gran does," the wife said, looking relieved. She nudged her husband. "Jamie here got a huge keeker when the Frazier lad come at him bleezin' in the pub." She drew a large circle in front of her own eye. "What you'd call a black eye, I reckon. My Gran's parsley and tea poultice took down the swelling in a snap."

The man scowled. "Aye, and it reeked like an alky's carpet, Deb." He handed Althea the receipt for her room charges, and asked, "Where are you off to now, Miss?"

She shouldered her carryall. "My next stop is the Isle of Skye, and then back to Glasgow."

"On Skye you'll no' be let near the Trotternish ridge," he said and nodded past her at the old television in the lobby, which was showing a newscast. "They barricaded all the trails last night after the Old Man of Storr crumbled. Naught but a pile of rubble left, they say."

"How terrible," Althea said. The rock formation was a popular tourist spot, and one of the most-photographed places in Scotland. "What caused it to collapse? An earthquake?"

"They dinnae ken yet," Deb told her. "But this rock expert they had 'round blamed a big sun surge that hit us before dawn. Something about the magnetics, wasn't it, Jamie?"

"Geomagnetics, and he called it a solar flare," her husband corrected. "It's meddled with the satellites, and disrupted electronics and signals all over the highlands. He said it's likely to last for hours, Miss, so your mobile may no' work until afternoon."

"Thanks for the warning," Althea said and smiled her good-bye to the couple.

She hadn't planned to visit the Storr while she was on the island. The ferns she wanted grew in a glen near the Black Cuillin. But the collapse would attract plenty of press. Cameras and reporters ranked at the top of her "Avoid" list.

Being the only child of dead rock stars had turned her into a media magnet for life.

Outside the inn Althea stowed the carryall in her rental car, and then walked down to have one last look at the loch. Behind the vivid ambers, oranges and scarlets of the autumn-painted trees the sky streamed with puffy ribbons of cloud. The dappled surface of the waters reflected the surrounding beauty like a master impressionist intent on capturing every hue. Since no one else was braving the early morning chill, Althea felt as if she had Scotland all to herself.

Wouldn't that be something? she thought, smiling a little. No towns or tourists, cars or roads—just her and nature, the way it used to be growing up on her uncle's farm. She'd been so happy there, away from her famous parents and the endless drama of their love-hate relationship.

As the founding members of the Nighthood, Will and Sharan Scarlet had headlined the world's most famous Gothic rock band. With their blazing red hair and tattered bohemian style, they had set trends all over the globe. But it had been Will's haunting lyrics and Sharan's operatic soprano that had catapulted them to the top. By the time their third album went triple-platinum, Will took his place among the top-selling songwriters of the century, while Sharan became a global idol and fashion icon as well as the most influential voice of her generation. Considered the most romantic couple in rock, the Scarlets had been utterly obsessed with each other.

The only hiccup in their epic love story performance had been Althea.

What the hell is this? Althea's mother had shrieked when she found the plane tickets to Georgia. *You're dumping the kid at your brother's place? Why?*

Will had bellowed right back at her. *Her name is Ally, and you can't take care of her, Shar. Christ, do you even look at her anymore? She's so thin I can count her ribs.*

She never wants to eat anything. Sharan had lit a cigarette and waved her beringed hand in the air. *Don't you blame me. The idiot roadies are supposed to feed her.*

So, we let the crew raise our daughter? What kind of mother are you?

Her mother's famous emerald-green eyes narrowed. *Like you're father of the year, you shit.*

As usual, the argument had escalated into a raucous, vicious fight, and ended with the Scarlets in the bedroom at the back of the tour bus. Althea remembered the details only because it was the last time she had seen her parents. Their studio manager took her from the bus and flew with her from Houston to Atlanta. From there he'd driven her to her uncle's farm in the heart of Georgia's dairy and logging country.

Gene Jarden turned out to be an older, leaner version of his brother, a lifelong bachelor, and a complete stranger to five-year-old Althea. After the Jarden's studio manager hurried off to catch his plane, the farmer had just stood there looking her over for a long time.

"You got a little of me, didn't you?" He crouched down so she could see the same, crystal-blue eyes she saw in the mirror every morning. "It'll be fine now, Althea. You just need a bit of fresh air and sunshine. You like peaches?"

Too terrified to say anything, she nodded.

Her uncle straightened and held out his hand. "Then you'd best come and help me pick some."

Gene's peach orchard covered three acres, and as they walked through the rows of the wide-topped trees with their blushing golden fruit he talked about the farm. He let her choose her peach, and lifted her up in his arms so she could pluck it off the branch. Althea couldn't remember ever doing anything like that. All she knew was that nothing before or since that day had tasted better than her first bite of that juicy, sun-warmed fruit. She wouldn't have become a botanist without her uncle and his orchard. Both of them had changed her life forever.

The sound of her smart phone ringing brought Althea back to the present, although when she saw who was calling on the display she frowned. She hadn't spoken to Gregory Davis since a year ago, when they'd gone their separate ways.

"Hello?"

"It's Greg. How's Inverness?" Without waiting for an answer, he said, "I'm flying to London today for a lecture series, and I heard you were over there. Any chance we could get together? I'm staying at Claridge's."

Throwing her phone in Loch Ness would be the most appropriate response, she thought. "London is a bit of a haul for a one-night stand."

"Same old Ally," her ex said, and chuckled. "Still as cold as ice. I swear, you've got liquid nitrogen for blood."

She hated being called Ally—another reason she'd broken it off with him. "Anything else before I hang up?"

"Yes. I want you back," Greg said. "I know you said no strings, but I thought we really had something, Ally. I miss you."

Althea imagined him reclined in the executive chair in his office, his tie loose and his dark blond hair falling over his smooth brow and dark brown eyes. He'd smell clean and warm, with a hint of the pricey cologne he liked to wear. By tonight she could be in that hotel bed with him, naked and enjoying his gym-toned body.

The problem was that she knew what the man actually wanted. For now, more sex, but also another chance to lure her into a relationship.

A traditionalist at heart, Greg would eventually talk her into marriage. After the honeymoon, he'd also persuade her to give up her work, so he could focus on his agritech career, where the real money was. In twenty years she imagined she'd have a lovely house, charity work, two kids in prep school, and a husband with the traditional mid-life crisis. He'd divorce her, buy a convertible, and move in with a lover young enough to be his daughter. Meanwhile, their kids would grow up and go.

Althea suspected she'd end up middle-aged and alone, with nothing to show but an empty nest and ruined dreams.

Althea would have told him that, too, but her uncle had taught her to be polite, particularly when she was this pissed off. "No, thank you. Enjoy your time in London." Her hand shook as she shut off the phone.

The anger slowly subsided as she walked back to the car. She hated when her emotions boiled over, but she couldn't blame Greg for this. Loneliness had driven her into his arms, but she'd lingered too long. Obviously he'd developed feelings and expectations she couldn't reciprocate.

Or maybe she was just over-reacting to what had been a transatlantic booty call, dressed up like a romantic appeal.

Althea didn't know. She never got emotionally involved with men. Oh, she'd always been passionate—sometimes to the point where she was overwhelmed by her own desires. Her self-imposed isolation brought on terrible bouts of loneliness, and she tried to channel her needs and frustrations into her work. Sometimes it wasn't enough, and she was tempted to do stupid things like her fling with Greg.

No doubt her lack of romantic interest did make her seem cold, but she needed that facade. It assured she wouldn't end up in some obsessive-abusive relationship like her parents. She had no intention of ever falling in love. Given her family history, she simply couldn't take the risk.

At least Althea had the work to keep her occupied. She touched the crystal heart pendant hidden under her shirt. A gift from her uncle for her sixteenth birthday, she'd worn it every day since his death. It reminded her of his love, and her calling.

With its endless woodlands, and the rare ferns they protected, Scotland had enormous potential for new finds. Today, she thought as she climbed into her rental, she'd discover something. Something that would make her forget that, without her uncle, she was alone in the world. She would focus on the work and, as usual, rely on herself.

• • • • •

Buy *Brennus (Immortal Highlander, Clan Skaraven Book 1)* Now

DO ME A FAVOR?

You can make a big difference.

Reviews are the most powerful tools I have when it comes to getting attention for my books. Much as I'd like it, I don't have the financial muscle of a New York publisher. I can't take out full page ads in the newspaper—not yet, anyway.

But I do have something much more powerful. It's something that those publishers would kill for: **a committed and loyal group of readers.**

Honest reviews of my books help bring them to the attention of other readers. If you've enjoyed this book I would so appreciate it if you could spend a few minutes leaving a review—any length you like.

Thank you so much!

MORE BOOKS BY HH

For a complete, up-to-date book list, visit HazelHunter.com/books.

Get notifications of new releases and special promotions by joining my newsletter!

Glossary

Here are some brief definitions to help you navigate the medieval world of the Immortal Highlanders.

Abyssinia - ancient Ethiopia

acolyte - novice druid in training

addled - confused

advenae - Roman citizen born of freed slave parents

Ægishjálmr - the Helm of Awe, a magical sigil

afterlife - what happens after death

ALS - acronym for amyotrophic lateral sclerosis, also known as Lou Gehrig's Disease

animus attentus - Latin for "listen closely"

apotheoses - highest points in the development of something

Anubis - the ancient Egyptian god of embalming and the dead

Aquilifer - standard bearer in a Roman legion

arse - ass

auld - old

Ave - Latin for "Hail"

aye - yes

bairn - child

Baltic – Scottish slang for very cold

banger - explosion

banshee in a bannock - making a mountain out of a molehill

barrow - wheelbarrow

bastart - bastard

bat - wooden paddle used to beat fabrics while laundering

battering ram - siege device used to force open barricaded entries and other fortifications

battle madness - Post Traumatic Stress Disorder

bawbag - scrotum

Belgia - Belgium

birlinn - medieval wooden boat propelled by sails and oars

blaeberry - European fruit that resembles the American blueberry blind - cover device

blood kin - genetic relatives

bonny - beautiful

boon - gift or favor

brambles - blackberry bushes

bran'y - brandy

Brank's bridle mask - iron muzzle in an iron framework that enclosed the head

Britannia - Latin for "Britain"

brownie - Scottish mythical benevolent spirit that aids in household tasks but does not wish to be seen

buckler - shield

Caledonia - ancient Scotland

caligae - type of hobnailed boots worn by the Roman legion

cannae - can't

cannel - cinnamon

canny - shrewd, sharp

catch-fire - secret and highly combustible Pritani compound that can only be extinguished by sand

Centurio - Latin for "Centurions"

century - Roman legion unit of 100 men

chatelaine - woman in charge of a large house

Chieftain - second highest-ranking position

within the clan; the head of a specific Pritani tribe

choil - unsharpened section of a knife just in front of the guard

Choosing Day - Pritani manhood ritual during which adolescent boys are tattooed and offer themselves to empowering spirits

chow - food

cistern - underground reservoir for storing rain water

claymore - two-edged broadsword

clout - strike

cohort - Roman legion tactical military unit of approximately 500 men

cold pantry - underground cache or room for the storage of foods to be kept cool

comely - attractive

conclave - druid ruling body

conclavist - member of the druid ruling body

conkers – horse chestnuts

contubernium - squad of eight men; the smallest Roman legion formation

COP - Command Observation Post

cosh - to bash or strike

couldnae - couldn't

counter - in the game of draughts, a checker

courses - menstrual cycle

cow - derogatory term for woman

Coz - cousin

craw - throat

croft - small rented farm

crucks - curved timber arches that support the thatched roof of a medieval cottage

cudgel - wooden club

cypher - a secret or disguised way to encode words

da - dad

daft - crazy

dappled - animal with darker spots on its coat

defendi altus - Latin for "defend high"

detail - military group assignment

dinnae - don't

dirk – a long-bladed dagger

disincarnate - commit suicide

diviner - someone who uses magic or extra sensory perception to locate things

doesnae - doesn't

dories - small boats used for ship to shore transport

dotterel - a small black and brown streaked wading bird

draughts - board game known as checkers in America

drawers - underpants

drivel - nonsense

drover - a person who moves herd animals over long distances

druidry - the practices of the druid faith

dung - feces

EDC - Every Day Carry, a type of knife

excavators - tunnel-diggers

fack - fuck

facking - fucking

falling vine - ivy

fankle – knot

faodail - lucky find

fash - feel upset or worried

fathom - understand

fere spectare - Latin for "about face"

ferret out - learn

festers - becomes infected

fetters - restraints

fibula - Roman brooch or pin for fastening clothes

filching - stealing

firesteel - a piece of metal used with flint to create sparks for fire-making fisher - boat

fishmonger - person who sells fish for food

floor-duster - Pritani slang for druid

flummoxed - perplexed, bewildered

foam-mouth - rabies

fougou – a stone-walled vault built underground for storage and other purposes

Francia - France

Francian - French

free traders - smugglers

frenzy - mindless, savagely aggressive, mass-attack behavior caused by starving undead smelling fresh blood

fripperies - showy or unnecessary ornament

gannet - a sea-diving bird

Germania - Germany

god-ridden - possessed

goldies - chanterelle mushrooms

Great Design - secret druid master plan

greyling - species of freshwater fish in the salmon family

gut rot - cancer of the bowel

hasnae - hasn't

heid doon arse up - battle command: head down, ass up

Hetlandensis - oldest version of the modern
name Shetland

Hispania - Roman name for the Iberian
peninsula (modern day Portugal and Spain)

hold - below decks, the interior of a ship

holk - type of medieval ship used on rivers and
close to coastlines as a barge

hoor - whore

huddy - stupid, idiotic

impetus - Latin for "attack"

incarnation - one of the many lifetimes of
a druid

isnae - isn't

itching pox - chicken pox

Janus - Roman god of duality

jeeked - extremely tired

Joe - GI Joe shortened, slang for American
soldier

jotunn - Norse mythic giantess

justness - justice

kelpie - water spirit of Scottish folklore, typi-
cally taking the form of a horse, reputed to
delight in the drowning of travelers

ken - know

kennings – compound expressions in Old
Norse poetry with metaphorical meanings

kirtle - one piece garment worn over
a smock

kona – Old Norse for woman

kuks - testicles

kyn-ligr – Old Norse for strange, wondrous

lad - boy

laird - lord

lapstrake - method of boat building where the
hull planks

leveret - baby hare

overlap

larder - pantry

lass - girl

league - distance measure of approximately
three miles

Legio nota Hispania - Latin name for The
Ninth Legion

loggia - open-side room or house extension
that is partially exposed to the outdoors

Losh – Scottish expletive meaning "Lord"

magic folk - druids

mam - mom

mannish - having characteristics of a man

mantle - loose, cape-like cloak worn over
garments

mayhap - maybe

Meus caparum Romanus, impetus - Latin for
"My Roman troops, attack"

milady - my lady

milord - my lord

missive - message

Moggy - Scottish slang for cat

mormaer - regional or provincial ruler, second
only to the Scottish king

motte - steep-sided man-made mound of soil
on which a castle was built

mustnae - must not

nattering - talking a great deal

naught - nothing

no' - not

Norrvegr - ancient Norway

Noto - Latin for "Attention"

oak-bast - woven oak fibers

Optia - rank created for female Roman
Legion recruit Fenella Ivar

Optio - second in command of a Roman
legion century

orachs - slang term for chanterelle mushrooms

orcharders - slang for orchard farmers

ovate - Celtic priest or natural philosopher

palfrey - docile horse

paludamentum - cloak or cape worn fastened

at one shoulder by Romans military commanders

parati - Latin for "ready"

parched - thirsty, dry

parlay - bargain

people of the black land - medieval term for ancient Egyptians

penchants - strong habits or preferences

perry - fermented pear juice

Pict - member of an ancient people inhabiting northern

pure done in – exhausted

Scotland in Roman times

pillion - seated behind a rider

pipes - bagpipes

pisspot - chamber pot, toilet

plumbed - explored the depth of

poppet - doll

poppy juice - opium

pottage - a thick, stew-like soup of meat and vegetables

pox-ridden - infected with syphilis

praefectus - Latin for "prefect"

prattling - talking too much and foolishly

Prefect - senior magistrate or governor in the ancient Roman world

Priapus - Roman god of fertility

Pritani - Britons (one of the people of southern Britain before or during Roman times)

privy - toilet

quim - woman's genitals

quinie – young woman

quoits - medieval game like modern ring toss

repulsus - Latin for "drive back"

remetch en Kermet - ancient Egyptians' name for themselves

rescue bird - search and rescue helicopter

retting - a process of soaking fibers in water to soften and separate them

roan - animal with mixed white and pigmented hairs

roo - to pluck loose wool from a sheep

rumble - fight

salr - Old Norse for a house consisting of one room

sandies - mussels

Sassenachs - Scottish term for English people

Saturnalia - Roman festival held in December to honor the god Saturn

scunner - source of irritation or strong dislike

sea stack - column of eroded cliff or shore rock standing in the sea

Seid - Norse magic ritual

selkie - mythical creature that resembles a seal in the water but assumes human form on land

Sekhmet - an ancient Egyptian warrior goddess who is an arbiter of justice

semat - undershirt

seneschal - steward or major-domo of a medieval great house

shield-maiden – a Norsewoman who choses to fight as a warrior

shouldnae - shouldn't

shroud - cloth used to wrap a corpse before burial

silver darlings - herring

skald – storyteller

skelp - strike, slap, or smack

skin work - tattoos

skuddie – naked

smalls - men's underwear

SoCal - slang for southern California

solar - rooms in a medieval castle that served as the family's private living and sleeping quarters

spellfire - magically-created flame

spellmark - visible trace left behind by the use of magic

spew - vomit

spindle - wooden rod used in spinning

squared - made right

stad - Scots Gaelic for "halt"

staunch weed - yarrow

stele - a tall, narrow slab of stone or wood

stupit - stupid

sun blight - a toxic form of algae

Svitiod - ancient Sweden

swain - young lover or suitor

swived - have sexual intercourse with

taobh - Scots Gaelic for "Flank"

tempest - storm

tester - canopy over a bed

the pox - smallpox

thickhead - dense person

thimblerig - shell game

thrawn - stubborn

tincture - a compound made of ingredients dissolved in alcohol

'tis - it is

'tisnt - it isn't

toadies - lackeys

tonsure - shaved crown of the head

torque – a metal neck ring

TP - toilet paper

traills - slaves

trencher - wooden platter for food

trews - trousers

trials - troubles

Tribune - Roman legionary officer

tuffet - low seat or footstool

turncoat - traitor

'twas - it was

'twere - it was

'twill - it will

'twould - it would

tyre – tire

Underground – Scottish subway system

Vesta - Roman goddess of the hearth

vind-áss - Orkney term for windlass, an appa-
ratus used for moving heavy weights

vole - small rodent related to the mouse

wand-waver - Pritani slang for druid

warband - group of warriors sent together on
a specific mission

wasnae - wasn't

water elf sickness – a medieval-era disease
now believed to be chicken pox, endocarditis,
or measles

wee - small

wench - girl or young woman

wenching - womanizing or chasing women for the purposes of seduction

white plague - tuberculosis

whoreson - insult; the son of a prostitute

widdershins - in a direction contrary to the sun's course, considered as unlucky; counter-clockwise.

willnae - will not

woad - plant with leaves that produce blue dye

wouldnae - would not

ye - you

yer – your

Pronunciation Guide

A selection of the more challenging words in the Immortal Highlander series.

Bhaltair Flen - BAHL-ter Flen
Bjarke Moller - YAR-kay MOH-lah
Black Cuillin - COO-lin
Cailean Lusk - KAH-len Luhsk
Catriona Haral - KAH-tree-oh-nah HAIR-ell
Daimh Haral - DIVE HAIR-ell
Dun Aran - doon AIR-uhn
Ennis Errol - IN-nus AIR-el
Evander Talorc - ee-VAN-der TAY-lork
faodail - FOOT-ill
Fiona Marphee - fee-O-nah MAR-fee
Iona Errol - ay-OH-nuh AIR-el
Isabeau - ee-SAH-bow

Isela Haral - ee-SELL-ah HAIR-ell

Kron Moller - KRAHN MOH-lah

Lachlan McDonnel - LOCK-lin
mik-DAH-nuhl

Loch Sìorraidh - Lock SEEO-rih

Neacal Uthar - NIK-ul OO-thar

Senga Errol - SEN-gah AIR-el

Seoc Talorc - SHOK TAY-lork

Silje Rowe - seel-JAY ROH

Tavish Haral - TAH-veesh HAIR-ell

Temmick Moller - TEM-mick MOH-lah

Teren - ter-INN

Tharaen Aber - theh-RAIN AY-burr

Thora Liefson - THOR-ah LEEF-sun

Tormod Liefson - TORE-mod LEEF-sun

Dedication

For Mr. H.

Copyright

Making Magic

❦❦❦

Welcome to Making Magic, a little section at the end of the book where I can give readers a glimpse at what I do. It's not edited and my launch team doesn't read it because it's kind of a last minute thing. Therefore typos will surely follow.

It's always a tricky thing to know when to end a series. But I've decided to end this one while it's strong and finish on a high point—at least I hope I am! It's been tremendous fun to write and is the best selling series I've ever had. So why stop?

There are a few reasons, but first and foremost is that change fuels creativity. Doing something new is the way to keep the fires of

story and character creation burning. Staying
with a series for too long risks my getting
repetitive and then me finding the writing
monotonous. However a close second is what's
sometimes called reader fatigue. It's that time
when you see a new book in the series is
coming but you don't care because it feels like
the overarching story will never really end.
You get tired of waiting to find out what's
really going on and how it will all end. And
finally, related to reader fatigue, is that point
when a series gets too long and new readers
are daunted. You look at the string of ten
books and think "do I really want to start
that?" I've experienced all of these are both a
writer and a reader. Although I know there are
some super long series out there, it's not something I aspire to. Don't get me wrong. If the
epic story comes along that demands to go on
and on, I'll have to write it. But for this series,
five feels like the right place to bring it to
a close.

But fear not. In Book 4 you may
remember Lachlan telling Kinley about a
group of legendary highlanders known as the
Skaraven. If I'm not mistaken—and how

could I be—we'll be seeing them up close and personal in the next series.

Thank you so much for making this series so wonderful for me! I'm super excited about the Skaraven so I hope you'll join me in those stories too.

Thank you for reading, thank you for reviewing, and I'll see you between the covers soon.

XOXO,

Hazel

Los Angeles, January 2018

Read Me

Like Me

Grab Another Book?